Beginning Again

Peggy Bird

CRIMSON
ROMANCE
Avon, Massachusetts

This edition published by
Crimson Romance
an imprint of F+W Media, Inc.
10151 Carver Road, Suite 200
Blue Ash, Ohio 45242

POD ISBN 10:1-4405-4406-9
POD ISBN 13: 978-1-4405-4406-4
ePub ISBN10: 1-4405-4405-0
ePub ISBN 13: 978-1-4405-4405-7
ePDF ISBN 10: 1-4405-4537-5
ePDF ISBN 13: 978-1-4405-4537-5

This is a work of fiction.

Names, characters, corporations, institutions, organizations, events, or locales in this novel are either the product of the author's imagination or, if real, used fictitiously. The resemblance of any character to actual persons (living or dead) is entirely coincidental.

Dedication

To Ginny Foster

Chapter 1

"What the hell are we doing?" Liz Fairchild didn't bother hiding her irritation from her ex-husband. "When I agreed to have lunch with you, I expected food and a martini, not a tour of Northwest Portland."

"Bombay Sapphire is good gin, but pouring it over a few ice cubes doesn't make it a martini," Mason Fairchild said with a grin, "even if you do throw in a couple olives. Although I've always been pretty sure you know that."

"Po-ta-to, po-tah-to." Dismissing his comment with a wave of her hand, she persisted. "Answer the question—where are we going?"

"You'll see in a minute. We're just about there." After maneuvering his Mercedes around a streetcar that had stopped to pick up passengers, he pulled into a small parking lot behind what looked like a row of townhomes, nosed the car into a parking space, and cut the engine. "This is it."

"And what would *it* be?"

"A live/work space a client of mine has on the market for a very attractive price."

"If I knew what a live/work space was, that might impress me. But I don't, so I'm back to wondering why I'm not sitting at your favorite restaurant with a martini in front of me."

"Patience has never been your virtue, has it?"

She pursed her mouth and cocked her head. "You of all people should know just how patient and understanding—"

"I apologize. You're right." He unfastened his seat belt and leaned over to unhook hers. "Just extend your understanding for another fifteen minutes and I promise there'll be gin in your very near future."

Although the dissolution of their marriage had been quite civilized, Liz was surprised when Mason called and suggested lunch. They had no reason to see each now that their divorce was final. But, curious about a business opportunity he said might interest her, she'd agreed.

She'd prepped for their lunch with almost as much care as she had for their wedding day. Her hairdresser cut and styled her hair so it looked fabulous, covering the few white invaders in her brunette waves with a subtle rinse. She wore her favorite silk suit—the one that matched her intensely green eyes—and a pair of expensive heels that made her legs look like they went on forever and let her tower over almost everyone in the room by adding three inches to her five-eleven height. She added a tennis bracelet and a diamond pendent Mason had given her. She wanted the look to say she felt great and was moving on, but didn't think unkindly of him. It was a lot to ask of a silk suit, a pair of shoes, and two pieces of jewelry but she thought she'd pulled it off.

However, the message was getting lost in her irritation and the dust of a parking lot in Northwest Portland. Peering through extremely dirty windows into a building she thought had all the earmarks of a chop shop for computers she said, "I thought your clients were small businesses about to go big. This looks like a junk shop."

"Don't let the mess fool you. The guy's a genius. He's doing something I don't understand with tablet computers and 'The Cloud.' " He put air quotes around the last two words. "He needs more space so he's moving into bigger facilities out in Washington County."

"And we're here because . . . ?"

"This space was an art gallery before he turned it into Portland's version of Steve Jobs's garage. I wondered if you'd be interested in buying it."

She was sure she looked as shocked as she felt. "Me? What would I do with it?"

"Use your art background to exhibit up-and-coming new artists, your exquisite taste to help clients figure out what to do with their living spaces, and your organizational skills to run a gallery/interior design business."

"You're joking. I've never run a business in my life."

"No, but I have and I've made quite a bit of money teaching other people how to do the same. I'll work with you. The least I can do now that I've wrecked your personal life is help you build a professional life that will make you happy."

"One of the things I have always liked about you, Mason, is your willingness to take responsibility for your actions." Liz put her hand through the crook of his arm as they walked around to the front of the building.

He leaned over and kissed her cheek. "You're a beautiful woman who was a superb wife. I hurt you by being unfaithful and by lying about who I was . . . who I am. I want to make what amends I can. I haven't given you any reason lately to believe me, but I do love you. Not the way you should be loved but . . ."

Shrugging off his apology, she interrupted, "It's done. Over. We both survived. And if you hadn't been trying to live a lie, I'd never have an investment account and an income anyone would envy. For that, I should be thanking you."

"And that's one of the things I've always loved about you. You're not only willing to face the unvarnished truth head on, you're quite likely to say it out loud." His laugh was warm and familiar.

"So, now that we have established our mutual admiration society, what's the deal with this space?" She stopped in front of a large display window on the street side of the building.

"It's a live/work space that—"

"Wait. I still don't know what a 'live/work space' is."

"It's exactly what it says: a place where you can both live and work. The second floor is a two-bedroom apartment that has access both from the downstairs workspace and the parking lot out back. It's small compared to what you're living in now—only 1,200 square feet, like the downstairs—and pretty basic. But you were thinking about selling the house anyway so maybe it would suit, at least in the short run."

When Liz tried to look through the window, she couldn't see much for the dust. With the help of Mason's handkerchief, she rubbed some of it away. Seeing the space more clearly didn't improve her opinion of it. "It looks like it would take a lot of work to make it habitable for an art gallery."

"It's really not that bad. Only the walls and floors need attention. Once my client gets his stuff out of here, you could—"

"Stop." Returning his handkerchief she said, "If you want me to listen to any more about this deal, we better get to the martinis. And it's plural now."

Over a two-martini lunch, Mason outlined why he thought an art gallery would work in the space and why he thought Liz was the right person to run it. At the end of his pitch he asked, "Why do you look so concerned? Surely you're not worried about money."

"It's not the money," she admitted. Their divorce settlement gave her enough cash to comfortably capitalize a small business. "It's everything else."

"Like what?" he asked.

She ticked off her objections and he countered every one. No experience running a business? He would take her on as a client to help her get it up and running. For free. A location with notoriously difficult parking? The streetcar ran close by; there was the small lot in the back and a larger one a block away. Hadn't the previous art gallery failed? No, the owner was so successful he moved to a larger space. How would she get clients in this bad economy? The adjacent shops that catered to the upscale neighborhoods nearby were doing well, and part of Mason's help would include a well-thought-out marketing plan. Expensive display equipment needed for a gallery? The original owner had left behind a hanging system and a storage unit full of pedestals.

Maybe it was Mason's enthusiasm and confidence that she was the right person to start this business, maybe it was the second martini, maybe she just ran out of reasons to oppose the idea but after almost three hours of talking, Liz agreed to look into it.

A month later, not only satisfied she could do it but excited about the possibilities of running a gallery, she signed the papers to transfer ownership of the building. The Fairchild Gallery was born.

Chapter 2

Liz decided to do the work of renovating her gallery herself for two reasons. The first was straightforward: She believed in sweat equity. The place wouldn't really be hers until she put some effort into it. So after she cleaned out a Dumpster-load of stuff the former owner left behind, she tackled the job of rehabbing the floors and walls herself. Every brushstroke, every pass of the sander across the floor made it more *hers*.

The second reason she was working ten-hour days was more complicated.

Mason had chosen the week before her forty-sixth birthday to announce that, although he loved her, he'd been hiding some important things from her. First, he'd been unfaithful to her throughout their marriage. Second, he'd fallen seriously in love so, third, he was leaving her for a younger man.

Alone, she'd "celebrated" being more than halfway through her forties. Over several martinis she contemplated the looming big 5-0, the subsequent descent into Medicare, the search for a doctor who'd accept government reimbursement at lower-than-cost levels from an old woman who lived alone with her cats. The need to acquire the cats.

This seemingly bottomless well of self-pity kept her occupied for several weeks after Mason turned her life upside down. Finally one Saturday, having neither dressed nor eaten all day, she decided it was time to do something other than wander aimlessly through her life. She began making lists of things to do.

First up, an embarrassing visit to her doctor to get a panel of tests for various STDs, all of which, thank God, were negative. Next, a divorce. That turned out to be easy. Mason wasn't about to fight her on anything. Her lawyer could have phoned it in, although Liz was sure she'd take credit for the size of the settlement. Mason's $7 million in assets, their residence in a community property state, and no prenup in place must have given her lawyer a hard-on just thinking about it. Assuming female attorneys got hard-ons. Or was the plural hards-on? Whichever, she was sure her lawyer had one, regardless of her sex.

The big one on the list, however, was what to do with herself. Although she didn't need a job for the money, she did need a purpose in life. Not easy for a midlife woman with an extremely dusty resume and a degree in art history to figure out.

The gallery was the answer to a prayer she hadn't even known she'd raised. Working to get it ready gave her a goal, an interest beyond herself, and more exercise than she'd had in years.

Mason helped. He guided her through developing a business plan and worked with her on an approach to marketing. He even suggested someone to help her do the renovations. His name was Jamie Bruce. He had the face of an angel and the body of a young god. She'd always liked pretty, young men and Jamie was certainly one of those.

He was also Mason's new partner.

Jamie had worked in IT for Mason's business, but left the company when they moved in together. Now at loose ends, he'd offered his assistance. At Mason's suggestion she'd accepted, mostly because her ex-husband was doing so much to help set up her business and she didn't want to look too dog-in-the-manger.

It turned out to be one of her better decisions. Jamie quickly made himself indispensible. Liz enjoyed his company and learned to value his opinion on types of art with which she had less experience than he did. She appreciated his willingness to help her with whatever needed to be done, from lugging pedestals and display cabinets out of storage, to priming the walls and moving heavy ladders around. And, thanks to his computer skills, she didn't have to struggle learning how to set up a website, a Facebook page, and a blog for the gallery—he did it for her.

When they'd finished refurbishing the gallery they started on the living space above. Liz had decided to move to avoid the traffic-choked commute across the Columbia River from Vancouver, Washington to Portland five days a week. When Jamie asked if she'd miss the big house she and Mason had lived in, she was surprised how quickly she said she wouldn't. She'd never really been comfortable in the 10,000 square feet of conspicuous consumption and wretched excess they'd shared. Oh, she loved their his-and-hers bedroom suites and the groomed lawn that sloped down to a dock on the Columbia River where they kept a couple boats, but even those things she could do without. The only thing she thought she might miss was her huge walk-in closet. She either had to pare down her wardrobe or build more closets in the apartment.

She put the house in Vancouver on the market and, in two days, sold it for $100,000 more than her asking price, thanks to a bidding war between two couples. The money was nice, but with it came pressure to get her new quarters ready and either sell the bulk of the furniture or put it in storage so the new owners could take possession.

With Jamie's help she got it done. Six weeks after she sold the house, she was living in Portland, in an apartment that reflected her taste alone. She'd brought some of her favorite pieces of furniture from the house in Vancouver, added a few new ones more to the scale of the apartment, and sprinkled the place with lots of rich colors—cobalt blue and deep gold pillows, red paisley-patterned throws, abstract paintings full of vivid splashes of yellow, green, and red—to replace the bland beige, blond, and cream palette she'd lived with for fifteen years because that's what Mason preferred. Moving in felt like coming home in all the best ways.

The opening of The Fairchild Gallery was set for October to give her time to put her PR campaign in place and to look for artists she liked. She found a half-dozen painters including one who specialized in oil portraits and a watercolorist who did delicate landscapes. A black-and-white photographer, several high-end jewelry makers, and a potter completed her starting lineup. Making the rounds of wholesalers, she gathered the information she needed for her interior design consulting. By the end of August, the big stuff was settled. All she had to do now was wade through a sea of details and she would be ready to open her business.

But like the rest of her life that year, things didn't go quite the way she'd planned.

Late one Friday afternoon, she was standing on a ladder checking the lightbulbs in the spots that had just been reinstalled. When she turned to climb down, she saw a man standing in the middle of the floor, his hands jammed into his jeans' pockets, looking around.

"I'm sorry, the gallery isn't open," she said, moving down a couple rungs on the ladder. "As you can see . . . "

"Yeah, I know you're not open." The man looked to be maybe four or five inches taller than she was. The worn jeans and faded UCLA sweatshirt he wore didn't disguise his slim hips and seriously luscious shoulders. When she gazed up from those shoulders, she saw a face that put him in his late twenties, thirty at most, in spite of the mop of prematurely white curls that fell sweetly around his ears and neck, except for the one in the middle of his forehead, cut, she was sure, to do exactly that.

Other than the hair around it, there was nothing sweet about his face. Not one feature was weak or recessive. Not the Roman nose or the sharply chiseled cheekbones and certainly not the strong jawline covered in a salt-and-pepper stubble that made his testosterone level unambiguously evident. Pure black eyebrows and long, dark lashes called attention to deep-set gray eyes half hidden under languorous lids.

When he raked those eyes over her, boldly inspecting her from head to foot and back up again, she involuntarily shivered at the charge she felt. He must have felt it, too. As his eyes swept back up to her face, they changed from merely gray to storm-at-sea. He straightened his shoulders and raised his chin as if to make sure he was presenting himself from a good angle.

Dear Lord, he was attractive. Hell, attractive was too weak a word. He was a walking thesaurus of adjectives for "magnetic." She couldn't remember the last time she'd paid such careful attention to a man. And she'd never before felt the jolt of electricity she experienced when their eyes met. Not only was she not offended by his frank appraisal of her, but she wished she'd worn something more flattering than black leggings and an oversized white shirt. When had she last thought about something like that? That was easy—never.

He stood looking at her, saying nothing.

She shook off her wandering lust. "If you knew the gallery was closed, why . . . "

"I always look at galleries when they're closed. Gives me a better feel for what they're about."

"But this one isn't just closed today." She waved at the empty walls. "I'm not even open for business yet."

"Yeah, I know. You're Liz Fairchild. You're new to the gallery business and you're going to open on First Thursday in October." His eyes swept over her again and the jolt of whatever-it-was reoccurred. "You really shouldn't wear black and white. You should wear intense colors. Emerald green. Cobalt blue. Something like that."

"How nice that you not only know who I am and what I should wear but what my business plans are." Was it her attraction to him or his arrogance that brought out that annoyed tone in her voice? "Who the hell are you, anyway?"

"Collins."

"Is that Mr. Something-Collins or Mr. Collins-Something?"

"Just Collins."

"And let me make a wild guess—you're an artist."

He seemed amused at her comment. "Yeah, I am."

"Well, *Just Collins*, if you're here to leave your portfolio I'd be happy to take a look at it, but I'm not sure . . . " She stepped off the ladder and regretted it. While on the ladder she was taller than he was, more in control, not so close to whatever charged field the man had around him.

"I don't leave my portfolio until I'm sure I'm in the right place for my work."

"And what would your work be?"

"I'm a sculptor. Metal sculptor." The amused look was still there.

"Sounds like what you do wouldn't work in this small space."

"I'm not looking for a place for my larger pieces. They're usually commissioned anyway, for public places or for some corporate hack who wants a big shiny thing in the lobby of his office. I'm looking for a gallery for my smaller pieces."

"I'm not hearing garden art here, am I?"

He snorted. "Yeah, right."

"As I started to say, you're welcome to leave your portfolio, but I'm not really looking for another three-dimensional artist right now. I'll give you my card." She started toward the back of the gallery to get a business card.

Suddenly he was standing next to her, reaching for her, putting his hand on her arm to detain her. She felt warmth through the sleeve of her cotton shirt and looked down, mesmerized by what she saw.

His hand could have been Michelangelo's model for the Sistine Chapel's Adam, reaching to God, or David's marble hand holding a slingshot. It was big and heavily veined, with long, slender fingers tipped by well-cared for nails and cuticles, not what she'd expect on the hands of a working sculptor. She wanted to take his hand, turn it over, feel the calluses she was sure were there, trace the lines in his palm before . . . before what? Closing her eyes, she tried to concentrate on something other than the sudden thought of having that hand and its partner someplace—anyplace—on her body where somehow she knew they would know exactly what to do.

She sucked in a breath, not sure what to do next. This never happened to her. Never. She wasn't a fluffy-headed girl. She was a grown woman who . . .

"Obviously, you've never seen my work." He took her hand in his. "I'll take you out to Clackamas on Saturday. The piece I did for the transit center there will be dedicated then."

She shook her hand loose before he could notice it was trembling. "I'm not sure where we're going with this conversation, but I think maybe you need to—"

"Have dinner with you tonight."

"Excuse me?"

"It's a little early, I know. But the gallery isn't open so you can leave. Let's go have a drink and something to eat. We can talk about my work and your gallery. And decide what time I can pick you up to take you out to Clackamas."

Not normally rendered speechless by anyone, Liz was at a loss for how to respond to this maddening yet somehow maddeningly attractive man. "Whether the gallery is open or not isn't the point. I rarely . . . no, let me amend that . . . I *never* go to dinner with someone I don't know."

A slow, very confident, smile made its way across his face. "But you'll make an exception for me, won't you?"

"Who do you think you are and why do you think I'll . . . ?"

"I told you already. My name's Collins. I could be your new

16

sculptor and I want to take you out for dinner so we can get to know each other. So, ready to go?" He took her hand again and brought it to his mouth, touching the tip of her index finger with his lips.

All of her senses were focused on the end of her finger as he nipped at it. When his mouth released her finger, he continued holding her hand. Those gray eyes, stormy with something she was afraid to name, looked deep into hers. But she knew he wasn't searching for an answer. He already knew the answer. He was looking to see if she was ready to admit she knew, too.

She took a breath, held it for a few seconds, and then let it out. "Give me five minutes to lock up," she said. "We can walk to the café down the block."

"I have my car. There's an Italian restaurant I like over on the east side. They have an excellent wine list. Do you like red or white wine?"

"Does it matter? If the decision about what we're drinking goes anything like the conversation we've had so far, you'll make up my mind for me."

His grin was smug, sexy, and amused, all at once. "You catch on quick. I like that in a woman."

*

Over drinks, she looked at his portfolio and saw just how gifted an artist he was. In spite of not immediately recognizing his name, she realized she'd seen his work, in several downtown office buildings and at an outdoor sculpture park. Any sane gallery owner would jump at the chance to represent him. So, being quite sane, at least up until now, she agreed he was her new sculptor.

She also learned that he'd been a partner in a Los Angeles law firm where he'd made a lot of money, but burned out from too many hundred-hour workweeks and too little time to do the art he really loved. Also, his hi-rise condo had a spectacular view, but no space for doing sculpture.

He'd moved to the northeastern part of Oregon, in the Wallowa Mountains, eighteen months ago so he'd have the time and space to create his art. His portfolio included images of his small, rustic cabin and the large, hi-tech studio he shared with another sculptor. He told Liz he only came to Portland three or four times a year, a fact that for some reason disappointed her.

In spite of her best efforts, however, she didn't learn the rest of his name. All he would tell her was that "Collins" was part of his birth name and the rest didn't matter.

By the time they'd finished dinner, dessert, and the bottle of a Brunello he'd selected, it was twilight. He paid with a platinum credit card, which, along with the late-model Porsche he drove, bolstered the story he'd told about being successful. Before he took her home, he arranged to pick her up at three on Saturday afternoon to accompany him to the dedication of his sculpture.

She couldn't remember anyone who'd bulldozed, manipulated, attracted, repelled, and confused her as much as Collins-with-no-other-name did. He was everything she hated in a man. Hell, in anyone.

So why she was looking forward to seeing him again?

Chapter 3

She wasn't what he'd expected. He'd been told she was "a tough old broad" who would give him a hard time and tolerate no nonsense. Okay, that last part was right. But old broad she wasn't. At most she was a couple years older than he was. And "broad" connoted a rode-hard-and-put-away-wet look that didn't come close to describing Liz Fairchild. She was all lean loveliness, grace, and long legs. Legs he wouldn't mind having wrapped around him. When they were both naked.

In those black leggings she looked like a dancer, a white Judith Jamison. Sexy, spirited, beautiful. Or maybe a taller Audrey Hepburn. Actually, her attitude was more like the other Hepburn's. With a slight change in accent she could pass for Katharine.

The surge of desire that had gone through him when he looked at her felt like the kick of a downed power line. It had been a long time since any woman had hit him that hard. That reaction was not helpful. He was supposed to be striking up this acquaintance to get information, not get her into bed.

Not that she was the usual type of woman who attracted him. Of course, his recent girlfriends in L.A. included a blond killer-shark lawyer and a purple-haired wannabe movie star who waited tables. Okay, maybe he didn't have a type. But if he did, he wouldn't have guessed it would be a tall, sexy, stubborn art gallery owner.

It was obvious Liz felt the same jolt when they met. The way she reacted when they'd locked eyes that first time was why she'd agreed to have dinner with him. He was quite sure she didn't go out with someone just because he asked.

Obviously she was damn smart. Which complicated what he was supposed to do. What he had to get out of doing because, after meeting her, after that jolt of attraction, he had other ideas about what he wanted from her.

He made a phone call as soon as he got back to his hotel room. "She's not what you told me to expect. I don't think I'll get what you want from her."

The man at the other end of the line said, "Look, Michael, our client says Liz Fairchild has the information. Your job is to figure out how to get it. Maybe she's pissed off enough at him to just give it to you. Maybe you'll have to search for it. But just do it."

"Something's not tracking for me. She's not some burned-out divorcée like the client said, she's . . . "

"What's that got to do with providing representation for our client? Are you using your big brain here or your little brain?"

"Stop saying *our* client. He's *your* client. And for fuck's sake, David, I don't look at every woman I meet as a potential bed partner."

"No, usually only the young and nubile ones. And Liz Fairchild's neither, I hear. Just get me the damn information and then sweet-talk her into bed if that floats your boat."

"I don't know . . . " Collins let the words hang there.

"Look, you owe me, man." David waited for a response. When none came, he said, "Besides, if you've got a thing for her, you'll have fun. She's bound to give in. There's not a woman alive who isn't susceptible to your renowned charm."

Collins sighed. "Okay, okay. You don't need to bullshit me. I'll see what I can find out. But when this is over, I'm done."

"Get me what I need and I won't bother you again."

***

On Saturday, Collins was waiting outside the gallery when Liz came downstairs. In place of his jeans and sweatshirt, he wore well-tailored gray trousers and a lightweight black jacket over a form-fitting black T-shirt that must have been silk, the way it clung to his pecs and abs. After what she'd seen of his artwork, she doubted he had to go to a gym to keep himself in shape. Just lugging around the materials would be exercise enough. And yet his sculpture had a delicate, soaring quality to it that belied the strength and weight of the metal with which he created it. That was what made it so marvelous.

But, in spite of what she kept trying to tell herself, she was more interested this afternoon in the artist than in his art. The look of approval in his eyes made her glad she'd taken care with what she was wearing—a pair of white slacks and a sleeveless shell of green she knew matched her eyes. Her sandals were expensive but modest and her silver chain and hoop earrings sterling.

"I'm glad you took my advice about wearing emerald green," he said.

"Oh, I just put on the first thing I grabbed from my closet," she lied.

He'd never know it took her twice as long to clean up the mess she'd made trying on half her clothes as it did to get dressed in what she'd finally selected.

The dedication was an eye-opener for Liz. The art gurus of Portland were out in force, fawning over Collins. She was almost embarrassed enough to leave when she thought about how she'd behaved when he came into her gallery. If she didn't recognize the name of one of the up-and-coming sculptors in the region, what the hell was she doing setting herself up in an art and design business?

When he introduced her as his Portland representative, more than one gallery owner who'd come to talk to Collins glared at her. Until then, she'd only intellectually understood the expression "if looks could kill." Had she been a lot younger, she knew exactly what they'd think she'd done to snag him for her gallery.

After the dedication, Collins made the rounds chatting up the politicians who were there. It intrigued Liz until it occurred to her that they were involved in selecting artists for public commissions and he was lobbying in the most subtle of ways. Impressed, she watched him move easily through both the art and political worlds.

Apparently there was no one this man couldn't charm, which made her feel slightly better at having been manipulated into attending the event.

Finally, the crowd thinned to only a few hangers-on, several of them young women who seemed interested in Collins personally, not artistically. After politely taking his leave of them, he said goodbye to the remaining art and political people and found her visiting with another gallery owner.

"Sorry it took so long. You ready to go, Liz?"

"You don't have to worry about me. I can catch a ride with Sophie." She indicated the woman sitting next to her.

"Didn't your mother teach you to leave with the guy who brought you?" he asked with a sly smile.

"She did. But she's not here to give me hell if I don't this one time."

Sophie Woods stood up. "I'm afraid you'll have to take your mother's advice, Liz. I'm driving down to Eugene to see my daughter, not back into Portland. Besides, if you don't give Collins cover, those groupies over there might attack. They seem to be circling, looking for a way in."

"See, I need you to protect me from bodily harm," he said.

"I have a feeling you can take care of yourself quite adequately. On the other hand, I wouldn't want to run the risk of letting you get injured before the ink even dries on our contract."

As they walked toward his car, his hand settled lightly on the small of her back. His touch was enough to make her feel dizzy.

His hand, his beautiful hand, was right above the curve of her bottom, heat seeping through the fabric of her clothes, radiating from her back to every cell in her body.

He opened the car door for her. She had her seatbelt fastened before she realized he was waiting for a response to something she hadn't heard. "Sorry, say that again?"

"I asked if you'd like to stop for something to eat. What were you woolgathering about?"

"Just appreciating being here. Maybe feeling a little embarrassed to find out half my competition would have killed to have you in their galleries and I gave you a hard time when you came into mine."

He was smiling—no, smirking—as he went to the other side of the car and got in. "Good. You owe me. I like it when the balance of power tilts in my favor."

"If I own . . . sorry, owe . . . you, do I get to pick where we eat tonight and pay?"

"Ignoring the Freudian slip, I guess it does. What's your pleasure? We can do anything you'd like."

Liz looked quickly at him and wasn't fooled by the innocent expression. The pleasure he was referring to wasn't gastronomic, she was sure.

She didn't know what she was going to do about that, so she pretended his comment was about dinner. "Well, as long as we're out here, how about Wong's King? They have great Chinese food and it's not far off I-205 on Division."

"Love good Chinese. You're on."

After another long dinner complete with an animated discussion about art and an exchange of who-had-traveled-where stories, they arrived at what Liz feared would be the awkward part of the day. They were back at her apartment.

He parked in front of the gallery and walked her to the back door at the foot of the steps that led up to her residence. She put the key in the lock and turned to him, holding out her hand, making it obvious she was going for a goodnight handshake.

"Thank you for including me today. I loved seeing your work."

"That's not why I asked you to go with me," he said, taking her hand and drawing her to him. "I wanted to spend time with you." He dipped his head; she could see the kiss coming.

She warded it off by putting her hand on his chest. "I don't think this is a good idea."

"I don't believe you." He tugged at her, to get her closer. "You reacted the same way I did the first time we looked at each other. It was electric—for both of us."

"I still don't think . . . ."

"There's your mistake, Liz. Don't think." He touched her lips softly with his mouth, a mere brush of a kiss, then his tongue lightly tasted her lower lip.

She shuddered. He smelled of an intoxicating mixture of something mostly citrus, a little spicy, and a whole lot male. It had been a long time since she'd smelled anything that good.

"See, when you don't think, it's a good idea." He tried to move closer but she backed away from him.

"No, it's not."

Shaking his head, he said, "Why isn't it a good idea to do what we both want to do?"

"First of all, I'm old enough to be your mother."

"You must have been very precocious. I'm thirty-eight and you're . . . what? Thirty-nine? Forty?"

"I'm forty-six and, okay, you're older than I thought you were. But I'm still a lot older than you are."

"Which made a difference when I was ten and you were eighteen. It doesn't matter now." He moved nearer. "We're adults, not kids, and we . . . "

"It still matters. You're one of my artists. It's not right."

"Oh, of course. You can seduce me for devious purposes. Or take advantage of my innocence. Wait. Didn't I sign a contract that keeps you from using me? And I'm an attorney, which pretty much eliminates any chance I'm innocent."

"Suppose my other artists find out and think I treat you better?"

"If your contracts won't keep you from doing something like that, I'd say your personality will." He put his hands on her waist and tried to pull her closer.

"Collins, I'm serious. This isn't going to happen. You need to get to your hotel anyway. You have a long drive tomorrow to get back to the Wallowas."

He stared at her, as if trying to decide if she meant it. Finally, he sighed. "Okay, sweetheart, you win. I won't try to persuade you to let me come upstairs." He cupped her face in one hand. "But surely that earns me a goodnight kiss."

He didn't give her a chance to say no. Brushing his lips across hers, he barely touched her. She'd thought every part of him was rock solid but that wasn't true. His mouth was soft, soft and sweet. The kiss was light and feathery and ended with him nibbling on her lower lip for a second or two. As he pulled away she felt relieved it hadn't been more complicated . . . and disappointed for the same reason.

Then he came back for more.

This time he was insistent, his mouth sensuous, not sweet. His tongue explored her lips, urging her to let him investigate further. She could feel the warm moisture of his mouth, couldn't keep a quiet moan from escaping as she felt herself respond. Her lips parted and he made a swift foray in, tangling his soft, velvety tongue with hers, promising what could be as he pulled her tight against him. His arousal was obvious. But just as the thought bubbled up through her brain that she had to stop this, he broke off the kiss.

"Goodnight, Liz." He touched her mouth with his index finger. "We'll continue this conversation later."

She took a deep breath before responding. "Ah . . . right. Later." Turning to open the door, she remembered why there would be a later and spun around. "Oh, wait. When will later be? I mean, when will you bring your work to me?"

"How about the Monday before your opening? Will that work for you?"

"Of course." She avoided his eyes as she asked, "Will you be here for the opening?" The half of her that wanted him to say "yes" battled with the other half, the part that hoped he'd just drop off his work and go back to the mountains.

"Wouldn't miss it. I'll be in Portland for a week at least. I have some business I need to take care of."

"Good. I mean it'll give me a chance . . . give us a chance . . . we can get your work set up so you're happy with it."

He smiled as if he understood exactly what it would give them a chance to do. "I can't imagine you doing anything but a good job of displaying it."

"Okay, so, I'll see you then. You have my number, my phone number," she clarified. "Call if you have a problem."

"Of course." He was standing so close she could feel his breath on her face.

Entering the hallway, she closed the door, took a deep breath, let it out in a sigh of relief, and went upstairs. She'd barely gotten to the top of the steps when her cell phone rang. It didn't take a genius, or caller ID, to know who it was.

"Yes, Collins?"

"You said to call if I had a problem," he said. "I have one."

"And what would that be?"

"I don't see my car. I think it might have been stolen."

She walked to the window, brushed the curtain aside and looked out. "It's right in front of the gallery where you left it.

But I don't see you."

"I'm in the parking lot, in the back. And I can't see my car. It's a problem."

"Did you forget how to get from the back of the building to the front?"

"Apparently. Considering that I can't come up there to get directions, why don't you come down and show me?"

She wasn't sure whether to laugh or yell at him. "Are you serious?"

"About you coming down here? Yes. About not knowing how to find my car? Maybe not so much. Just come back down for a minute, please?"

She hesitated, sure she'd regret going downstairs, but knowing she was about to anyway. "All right. If that'll get you on your way."

When she opened the door, he took her hand and held it firmly as they walked around the building.

"Oh," he said when they got to the street. "There it is."

He punched the button on his remote and she heard the door unlock. She shook her head. "What the hell is this about, Collins?"

"This," he said, pushing her up against the side of the car. "It's about this." He took her in his arms and pinned her with his body. Taking control of her mouth, kissing her as if he wanted that more than he wanted to breathe, his tongue tasted every inch of her mouth. His hands skimmed her hips, dipped in at her waist, then moved up to the sides of her breasts. His thumbs circled both nipples. She could feel them harden, feel the heat and dampness between her legs that he raised in her. Oh, God, did he knew how to kiss, how to hold her. This was more like her fantasy of kissing than her actual experience.

Her arms seemed to develop a will of their own and went around his neck as her body arched into his, pressing her breasts against his chest, wanting those hands to . . . to what? To move down her hips to her bottom and pull her tighter against his erection so she could feel him, hard and aroused. The thought had no sooner shot through her mind than he did it.

If he could read her thoughts, she was in trouble. Deep, deep trouble. She had to stop him before it went any further.

But he acted first, letting her go, moving slightly away from her but keeping his hands on her waist. "I needed one more kiss before I left." He turned toward the car, then back again. "Well, maybe two more." This one, like the first kiss, was sweet and gentle. "There, now it's really goodnight. I promise." He kissed the end of her nose. "No, I guess that's it."

She stood rooted to the sidewalk as he started the engine and put the car in gear. Before he pulled out he said, "Breakfast tomorrow at nine. Okay?" and left without waiting for her answer.

Chapter 4

Her buzzer rang the next morning at nine. Collins wasn't anywhere near the freeway driving east, out of her life until she figured out a way to manage him or at least manage her reaction to him. He was at her door, a coffee carrier in one hand and multiple Starbucks bags in the other.

"I thought you were going back to your cabin," she said as she let him in. "And," indicating the sacks, "who the hell is coming to breakfast that you brought all that?"

"Couldn't decide what pastry you'd like so I brought two of everything they had." He followed her to the kitchen where he began searching her cabinets until he found an acceptable plate on which to put a wild assortment of muffins, scones, bagels, and coffeecake.

"I took a chance that you were a latte kinda woman. Hope I was right." He removed a large cup from the cardboard carrier and handed it to her. "And I have two juices for you to choose from." He placed three containers on the table along with a couple of glasses he took from the cabinet before motioning for her to sit.

She hesitated a moment, then pulled out a chair. She hadn't eaten yet and it looked good. What harm could there be in having breakfast with the man? After all, he was leaving as soon as they finished. Wasn't he?

"Back to my original question. Aren't you leaving for home today?" She opened a bottle of pomegranate and blueberry juice and poured it into a glass.

"Aha. I *knew* you'd be an antioxidant freak like me. I should have just gone with that and left the oj behind." He snatched up the second container of the same juice and drank from the bottle. Wiping his mouth on a napkin he pulled from a bag, he

29

winked at her. "I've decided not to leave for a couple days. I'm having too much fun here."

Her heart surged, then sank. That was the harm in eating breakfast with him. It was going to lead to . . . to who knows what? Dear God, what was she going to do?

As if responding to her unspoken question, he said, "I thought we should get to know each other a little better. Hang out, eat dinner, that kind of thing. No pressure. Just an artist and his representative."

She almost snorted the juice out her nose. "No pressure? Collins, how dumb do you think I am?"

"I don't think you're dumb at all. Quite the opposite. You're way too smart for me. The point of this is for you to get to know me."

"Does anyone ever say no to you and you take it as no?"

"Lots of people. Judges, juries—in both my legal and art careers, newspaper critics."

"I'm thinking more in the personal arena."

"There, too. But when a woman kisses me the way you did, I have hopes."

"That was just a weak moment . . . "

He hoisted the juice container in a toast. "Then here's to more weak moments." After downing the rest of the juice, he pushed the plate of breakfast treats towards her. "You first."

Her hand hovered over the plate. He grabbed it before she could make a choice.

"No, wait. I have a better idea. Let me see if I can figure out what you'll pick." He watched her closely, then looked at the plate, then back at her face. "Okay, you keep looking at that scone with the icing on top. *But* even though you want that one you'll take something else because you think the icing isn't good for you. So, you'll go for the bagel. Later, after I'm gone, you'll pick the icing off the scone and eat it." He released her hand and sat back in the chair.

She jerked her hand away from the bagel she'd been about to take and selected a blueberry muffin instead.

"You weren't going to take that muffin and you know it." He laughed and picked up the rejected bagel. "So, when we finish breakfast, what shall we do today?"

"I have work to do in my gallery. In case you've forgotten, I'm trying to start a business."

"It's Sunday, Liz. You deserve a day off. How about we go to the zoo?"

"The zoo? That's your idea of getting-to-know-you activities?"

"You can tell a lot about a person by the kinds of animals she likes."

*

It turned out, he was right. She wanted to go immediately to see the giraffes, which she said she had some sympathy for, whereas he wanted to see the elephants because he was always hoping he could find a way to free them from the confinement of their tiny cage. Neither of them liked to watch the sea lion who swam the same circle in its small tank like a patient pacing the floor in a psychiatric ward. They agreed that the big cats were beautiful to watch and the lorikeets annoying when they buzzed you looking for food.

Mid-afternoon, when he dropped her off at home, he said he'd be back at seven to take her out for dinner at a place he wanted to try in the trendy Pearl District. Because she'd given up fighting about his planning her day, she agreed.

When he arrived, he had a bottle of wine with him.

"I thought we were going out."

"We are. But I couldn't get a reservation until 8:30 so I thought we could have a glass of champagne here. You like champagne, don't you?"

"I love it. And you even brought my favorite, Argyle. But it's not really champagne."

"Hey, who's the lawyer here? I know it's technically sparkling wine, but what the hell? I don't see any French wine police around to object, do you?" When she shook her head he said, "Okay, then, how about glasses for this not-champagne?"

"Right here," she answered, bringing out two crystal flutes and an ice bucket to keep the bottle chilled.

They settled on the couch in her living room.

"So, now that we know each other better . . . " he started.

"One trip to the zoo and we know each other better?"

"Absolutely. Now that we know each other better, I want to revisit our conversation from last night."

"Which one?" Her mind was whirling trying to find an escape, any escape from the topic he was about to raise. The only result was dizziness from the effort.

"Do you really need to ask?"

"That's a closed topic, Collins. There's nothing more to say."

"Oh, I think there's a whole hell of a lot more to say."

"All right then, if you insist, let me be blunt, since subtle seems to be lost on you. We're not going to get involved the way you're suggesting."

"Why not? I can't believe you don't want to. I saw your face. I know how you felt when we kissed. And the age and contract excuses are bogus. I'm sure of it. What's it really?"

"Look, I'm no good at it, all right?" She avoided his eyes, putting her head back on the couch and staring at the ceiling. "There's no point in going any further because it'll be awful for you and then I'll be embarrassed and feel like a failure and we'll never be able to have a decent conversation about anything ever again and . . . "

"You're no good at it . . . at what, exactly?"

She sighed and closed her eyes, hoping she could get it out without having to look at him. "At what you want. I'm . . . I don't know . . . lacking in skills, grace. Whatever it takes to be a good lover, I don't have it. I never have. So it's better not to even . . . "

"Who the hell told you that?"

Her eyes flew open and she finally looked at him. "No one had to tell me. It's been obvious."

"So . . . what . . . you don't like sex?"

"Of course I like sex. It's nice. Sex is nice."

"Babe, sex can be hot and sweaty or breathtaking and amazing, sometimes it's off the charts sensational or even fun, but it sure as hell isn't *nice*. Tea parties are nice. If that's what your experience has been . . . "

"That's what I'm trying to say. I'm bad at it."

"More likely you've been with men who didn't know what they were doing."

"And, of course, you do."

"You won't know until you try, will you?"

She shook her head. "You are the most arrogant, conceited, egotistical man I've ever met. Is there anything you don't think you do well?"

"We can have a discussion of my character flaws another time. Tonight, we're talking about you." He smiled. "Hell, I thought you were going to tell me you had a contagious disease or were dying or belonged to some religion that requires celibacy. What you're talking about is just a little delusion. We can take care of that." He furrowed his brow, as if considering how to accomplish the task.

"A delusion? I'm deluded? Do you have any idea how hard it was for me to tell you that? And you brush it off as a delusion." She sat up straight with her arms crossed over her chest. She was sure fire was shooting out of her ears or maybe her nostrils. "And I'm not something you 'take care of.' I'm not a project."

"God, no, you're not. You're a beautiful woman who found the switch to turn me on the first time she looked at me, but

33

who thinks she's frigid or something."

"I didn't say I was frigid. I said I was inept. And is this your idea of no pressure? This is about as high pressure as . . . as . . . . I can't even think of anything that's as high pressure as this conversation is." She put her glass down on the coffee table. "This was not a good idea." She moved away from him, perched on the edge of the couch for a moment, and started to get up.

He took her hand to stop her. "Wait. I'm sorry. I'm pushing when I promised not to."

"It's too late. I think the evening's over."

"But we haven't had dinner yet."

"Dinner? After this conversation?"

"Aren't you hungry? I am. That hot dog we had at the zoo wasn't very much." He kissed the back of her hand. "Come on, Liz. I know you want to try this restaurant. I hear it's great. Don't take it out on the poor restaurant because I've been an idiot."

She shook off his touch. "You are the most maddening man—person—I've ever met. Why do I keep giving in to you?"

He shrugged. "My mother says I'm cute. Maybe that's it."

*

The restaurant was everything they'd both heard it to be—trendy, expensive, and good. When they arrived, the owner, Tom Webster, after ascertaining that the Collins on the reservation list was indeed the well-known sculptor, welcomed them and brought them a bottle of wine compliments of the house. Webster was a tall, good-looking man who oozed fake charm. At least that's what Liz thought. She might have been influenced by the way he hovered over Collins, ignoring her. When he finally acknowledged her it was to give her his advice on how to make her business better—even though he'd never been in her as-yet-unfinished gallery.

He wrapped up his list with a suggestion that she feature a woman he knew who did some kind of glass art—Liz was convinced it was collapsing wine bottles in a kiln to make cheese plates—and promised that he'd allow some of her artists to display in his restaurant once she'd proven herself a success. She listened politely, grinding down her molars a bit and trying not to spit at the man. When he left to bother other patrons, Collins, whose sly smile suggested he'd been enjoying the exchange, poured the wine from his glass into hers, saying she needed it more than he did.

Local politics absorbed their attention through their entrees, but when dessert was served, Collins brought the conversation back to something more personal.

"So, you've been married?" he asked.

"Yes."

"Want to tell me about it?"

"Why would I?" She squirmed in her seat.

"So we get to know each other better."

"I thought we were finished with that experiment."

He leaned across the table and held out a forkful of his chocolate cake for her to taste. "You said we were finished with it. I'm not ready to give up on it yet."

Licking the icing off her mouth, she said, "I'm still eating. Why don't you go first? Have you been married?"

"Not even close. I decided a long time ago that marriage wasn't likely to be in my future. The reasons people get married seem to be to have live-in company, kids, or both. I'm a workaholic who likes being alone when I'm not working, and the responsibility of raising a child to be a decent human being scares the bejesus out of me."

She was amazed at how easily he talked about something so personal. He didn't even need prodding to continue.

"I've had a couple long-term relationships, one in my twenties and one in my early thirties. Both ended when the women wanted what I couldn't give them—the house with the white picket fence, the 2.3 kids, the golden retriever named Honey. So we parted friends. Sort of. When I want company, I can usually find someone to go to dinner with me. Or whatever. And I know lots of people with ideas about who to fix me up with if I can't find someone on my own." He sat back in his chair and sipped his coffee. "That's my story. What's yours?"

"It takes a bit longer."

"We have the rest of the night."

She hesitated, not sure exactly what to tell him. Then the thought occurred that the truth might be what she needed to take control over what the hell was happening between them. So, he'd get the truth. The whole truth.

"When you were eleven and I was nineteen . . . " She ignored the interruption of a raised eyebrow and a theatrical cough and plowed ahead. "When I was nineteen, I married one of my college professors. He was forty-three. I was this hick kid from the Central Valley in California and he was the most sophisticated man I'd ever met. I thought he loved me." She sighed. "Turned out, he was looking for a research project not a wife."

"He was Henry Higgins and you were Eliza Doolittle?"

"Except, unlike in *My Fair Lady*, he never got emotionally attached. We married just before his sabbatical year and I dropped out of school to travel with him. He tutored me in art at some of the most famous museums in the world. Those places I talked about visiting at dinner last night? Roger took me to most of them."

"What happened to him?

"Fast forward about five years of my struggling—not always successfully—to be a good faculty wife. I hear a strange noise in the bathroom one morning when he was shaving. He'd collapsed. Didn't survive the ride to the ER. Massive heart attack."

"No kids?"

"He had two sons from his first marriage, both older than me. He didn't want more. Each of his children—and he clearly counted me in that group—got a third of his estate. He'd done well from the books he'd written and invested wisely, so I had a modest financial cushion at a young age."

"What'd you do?"

"I got a job with the development department at the county art museum and hid there for five years or so while I took a few classes every semester until I finished my degree. Never really dated anyone until I met Mason Fairchild at a museum fundraiser a few months after I'd graduated. Six months later, we were married."

"Please don't tell me he was twenty-five years older than you."

"No, only ten."

"And you loved each other?"

"Yes, in some ways we still do. We had a good marriage, I thought. Well, I wanted kids and he didn't, but then I had surgery and couldn't anyway so . . . " She held up her hand to ward off the question she knew was coming. "Before you ask, what happened was, early this year he came out of the closet and went off with a younger guy."

Collins didn't say anything, just took her hand and stroked it with his thumb. The display of silent tenderness brought a few sudden tears that she blinked back hard before continuing. "I was married to two good men and it didn't work with either of them, in any way. Obviously, I don't know what the hell I'm doing when it comes to men. So I'm done. Besides, at my age . . . "

"You're a beautiful, smart, sexy woman. Of any age."

"Sexy? When the men I've been with didn't care to have sex with me? Really?"

"And this conclusion is based on what . . . ? Your extensive survey of men, which consists of a husband twice your age who viewed you as a child and a closeted gay man? Or are you hiding a laundry list of other lovers?"

She looked across the table at him, expecting to see amusement or ridicule. Instead she saw what she'd seen before. Affection. Attraction. Something that frightened her but she didn't know why. "It doesn't matter anyway. I have no intention of getting close enough to rely on any man for anything other than a social conversation. It's too complicated."

"Complicated but fun."

She motioned to the waiter for the check. "Fun is getting my art gallery in shape for the opening. And I have to get back to that tomorrow. So I think I'll call it a night."

Collins snagged the check from the waiter before she could. "Can I help you do whatever you need to do?"

"Thanks, but I have someone working with me. He'll be in tomorrow."

"I thought you weren't going to rely on a man again." His sly smile was back.

"He's an exception. Besides, even if I was his type, he's unavailable."

Chapter 5

The ride home was quiet, Collins intent on driving, Liz trying to anticipate what his next move would be. She was sure there would be one.

She was right. When they got to her apartment, before she could get out of the car, he patted down various pockets as if looking for something. "I think I left my phone upstairs. Mind if I go up with you and look for it? And maybe we can finish the bottle of not-champagne."

"Tell me where you think you left it and I'll go look. And I've had enough wine tonight, thanks."

"Then, how about a cup of coffee or something? That won't ruin your schedule for tomorrow, will it?"

She didn't answer immediately, torn, she had to admit, between wanting him to stay, willing him to go, and not understanding why she had both reactions within five seconds of each other. "A cup of coffee or something. For a half-hour. Then you'll leave."

"I'm a big fan of 'or something.' And if you still want me to go after a half-hour, I will."

He followed her up the steps and into the kitchen. Before she could ask if he wanted decaf or regular, he pulled her into his arms, buried his face in her neck, and began kissing his way up to her mouth.

"Collins, please . . . " She half-heartedly pushed at his chest but he persisted, taking tiny nips at her mouth.

"Please, what, sweetheart? This, maybe?" Without waiting for a response, he took possession of her mouth with such authority she was breathless. The kiss took all the air from her lungs and turned her insides to liquid. She couldn't move.

Somehow her arms snaked their way around him as he pulled

her tight against his body. Her hands buried themselves in the curls at the back of his head. Her mouth returned his kiss, her tongue tasting him, exploring his mouth as thoroughly as his explored hers.

He slid his hands down her back and snugged her hips against his, fitting his erection into the V between her thighs. She moved to accommodate him and he pressed closer. Even through the layers of their clothes she could feel him get harder. She couldn't suppress a moan, couldn't stop her treacherous body from melting against him, from getting wet and feeling needy. She had to stop him . . . but oh, God, she didn't want to.

He broke the kiss and she tried to pull away. "Collins, please. You have to listen. This can't happen. You'll be disappointed."

"When you kiss me like that? Sweetheart, how could I be disappointed? And believe me, I'm paying attention—to your mouth." He touched her lips with his. "Your body." The palm of his hand grazed the tight, hard tips of her nipples. "Your arms." He wouldn't let her withdraw them from his shoulders. "Your body's saying what we both want to hear. The only part of you that's afraid is between your ears."

"I'm not afraid," she gritted out through clenched teeth.

"Show me. Come sit on the couch with me."

She could barely hear him as he nuzzled her neck. "The coffee . . ."

"Can wait. You said a half-hour and coffee or something. I'm picking 'or something.' And by my watch," he looked at his bare left wrist, "I still have about twenty-five minutes." He took her hand. "Come on, babe."

"And what," she asked as he led her to the living room, "do you think this will accomplish?"

"After a little bit, I think you'll suggest we see why I don't think sex is 'nice.' Are you brave enough to try?" He grinned at her. "Better yet, to bet?"

"Bet? On what?"

"I bet when we make love, you'll admit that it wasn't nice."

"Why do you think we'll . . . ?" She shook her head, trying to make sense of what was happening. "Why will I . . . if we did that . . . which we won't . . . why will I think it isn't nice?"

"Because it'll be amazing. Twenty bucks?"

She looked at the expression on his face and felt the jolt of electricity he sent through her every time those gray eyes held onto hers. She licked her lips at the thought of how his mouth tasted, the way her body responded when he kissed her. She had no idea why it happened, how it happened. All she knew was he affected her as no man ever had before. "I've never bet on sex . . ."

"Let me be your first, then." He feathered a kiss across her lips and she shivered. "Although, fair warning, I expect to win an easy twenty bucks," he said softly.

Taking her face again in his hands, he held her gaze for a long moment, stroking her cheeks with the pads of his thumbs. "God, you're beautiful. Beautiful and sexy and smart and funny and all the things any man could ever want in a woman."

He outlined her cheekbones, her eyebrows, the sides of her nose with his fingertips. "All the things I want in a woman." As his hands neared her mouth, she felt her breathing kick up a notch, felt a swirl of desire skitter through her body. When he finally kissed her, it was familiar, somehow, the taste of him. She'd kissed him for the first time yesterday and yet he tasted like the place where she'd always belonged.

She sighed as he raised the heat in the kiss. The slight suction of his mouth took the rest of her breath away. At least, she thought that's what happened. Why else would it feel like there was so little oxygen in her brain? Was that why she felt dizzy, like she was floating someplace outside herself?

While she was trying to figure it out, his hands, his beautiful hands, were making their way around her body, feeling just as incredible as she'd thought they would. He slid them up under her shirt and found her breasts, cupping and caressing them, gently at first but more urgently as her nipples hardened into diamond points.

The swirl of desire she'd felt had now moved south and found residence in her lower belly. The longer he kissed her, the more heavy and languid her limbs felt. A liquid heat spread through her body.

He tugged at the hem of her shirt, pulling it up over her head, then put her hands on the hem of his T-shirt, helping her strip it off him. When they were both naked from the waist up, he lowered her back onto the couch and positioned himself between her legs with their bare torsos against each other. "Now this I agree is nice, sweetheart," he whispered as he held her for a moment. "Just like this, skin on skin." He moved his hands up her body until he reached her face. "I love touching you. You're so soft and smooth."

Lowering his head, he began to tease and torment her breasts with his mouth, raking his teeth gently over her nipples, then suckling at them. No one had ever concentrated on them so lovingly, so lavishly. She'd always been embarrassed by her small breasts. She'd never known they could be so sensitive to a man's attention, could ache for the feel of his mouth. When she arched towards him and her breathing stuttered, he said, "You like this, do you?"

"Mmmm," was all she could manage.

"You'll tell me if I do anything you don't like?" His gray eyes had become black with desire, but the expression on his face was serious. He meant it.

"Mmmm."

A smile now. "That's 'yes,' I take it?"

"Mmmm."

"Let's see if you like this," he said as he moved down her body with hot, wet, open-mouth kisses. When he got to the waistband of her pants, he paused, raised his head and watched her as he moved one hand slowly, slowly, down, down to the place between her thighs that was hot and achy and very, very damp. He cupped her sex through her clothes and began to gently rub the side of his hand against her.

"Mmmm . . . that feels so . . . . . . "

"So what, sweetheart?" His replaced his hand with his erection and rocked his hips into her.

"So good. It's so good."

Her hands had begun to explore his chest, his shoulders, his back and arms, feeling the movement and strain of his muscles as his hands roamed over her body, teasing her breasts, massaging her belly. He was all solid muscle covered in hot skin, unlike any man she'd ever caressed like this. When he moved his hips against her, she gripped his buttocks and pulled him closer, wanting more of the long, hard length of him she could feel pressed against her.

Her brain was flooded with sensations from her skin, her breasts, from every place he touched—wonderful sensations. She kissed him back with an intensity she didn't know she was capable of, feeling as intoxicated as she would from downing martinis on an empty stomach.

And she wanted more.

"Collins, wait . . . " She stopped his hand as he insinuated it under the waistband of her slacks.

"Not tonight, babe. No more waiting."

She sighed. "I know. But not on this couch. Can we go someplace more comfortable? Like my bedroom?"

He pulled back and grinned. It was the most lascivious expression she'd ever seen. "When we get there, can I take off the rest of your clothes?"

"What would be the point of being in bed half-dressed?"

He laughed out loud. "God, you're wonderful, Liz. You may take a while to get there but when you do . . . "

She pushed at his chest and he rolled off the couch. "You better stop laughing at me or I'll change my mind."

He stood and held out his hand to help her up. "No, not *at* you, sweetheart, *with* you."

As soon as they got into her bedroom, she stripped down to her white lacy bikini panties and he to his black silk boxers. He clicked on the light by the side of the bed.

"Don't. Leave it off, please," she said as she reached for the light switch.

"I want to look at you. I want to see your face when you come." He brushed her hand away and sat her down on the bed.

She crossed her arms over her breasts. "I don't know that I want you to look at me like that. I'm not some twenty-year-old."

"You're beautiful and age is only a number."

"Maybe we should . . . "

"Maybe we should finish what we've started. And don't tell me any more sad stories about how I'll hate it in bed with you. This tells me otherwise." He took one of her hands and pressed it around the erection that was tenting up the front of his boxers.

She jerked her hand back as if it had been scorched. My God, he was big everyplace, wasn't he? As she scuttled into the middle of the bed, she wondered what she had gotten herself into. And what was about to get into her.

He pulled the comforter and sheets down and wordlessly urged her under them. His eyes were smoky with desire, which somehow both comforted and exhilarated her. How he could calm and arouse her at the same time was a mystery she would have to solve later. But not now. Right now she had to concentrate on storing up oxygen for when he kissed her again.

And figure out why he wasn't joining her in bed. As she

watched, he felt around in the pocket of the trousers he'd shed and she realized what he was doing. "You don't need a condom. I can't get pregnant and I just had tests for everything imaginable. They were all negative and I haven't been with anyone since."

"And you're not worried about me? What I might have?"

She looked at him with unblinking eyes. "If you say you're okay, I believe you. I trust you. If I didn't, you'd never have gotten into my apartment, let alone my bed."

He hesitated so long, avoiding her gaze, she began to wonder if he was having second thoughts. Or didn't believe her.

Finally he swallowed hard and said, "I'm not sure I'm that deserving, but thank you. I am okay."

What did he mean, he wasn't deserving? It was out of character for the Collins she'd seen so far. Her desire-clouded mind struggled to make sense of it. Before she could, however, he shed his boxers and knelt over her saying, "So, where were we?" and she forgot what she was supposed to be figuring out.

His legs astride her and with a wicked smile on his face, he slid his fingers under the waistband of her bikinis and began to slip them down over her hips, seeming to enjoy the way she squirmed as he touched her. When he'd gotten the panties off, he moved slowly, kissing as he went, back up her body until he was where he had been when they were on the couch, his legs between hers, his erection tight against the cleft of her sex, his arms braced on either side of her chest. His mouth hovered over hers and he whispered, "We were about here, I think."

"Oh, God . . . I think . . . yes, that's . . . it's exactly where we were."

But they didn't stay there for long. As he resumed his ministrations to her breasts, and the kisses that robbed her of a will to be anyplace but here, her body began to feel restless, demanding more from him. A desire she'd never felt before began building deep in her, confusing her with the intensity, exciting her with the power.

He seemed to understand and left off kissing her mouth and began to move down her body again, kissing, nipping, and licking between her breasts, to her navel, her hipbones. When he got to her sex, he used his tongue to tease again, this time the nub of nerves where the coil of heat had taken up permanent residence. He began slowly circling, then rapidly flicking the tip of his tongue across her clitoris as her hips bucked up to give him more access.

She'd never felt anything like it, this electricity racing through her body, this need to have him inside her, to be completely his. No one had ever made love to her like this before. She whimpered in protest when he moved his mouth only to gasp with pleasure as he introduced his fingers into her slick, tight channel.

His fingers moved inside her, finding a place she didn't know existed and massaging it as his thumb circled her clitoris. The orgasm ripped through her and she knew the world would never be the same again.

"Collins, please . . . " She tugged at him to move up, so she had contact with more of his body.

"Please, what, sweetheart? Tell me what you want. I'll do whatever you want me to. Just tell me."

"I want you."

"How? How do you want me?" He moved up over her, his body rubbing against hers with the maximum of friction, every inch of her body aware of every inch of his.

"Inside me. Please."

"Like this?" She could feel his finger moving inside her.

"No, I want . . . " She paused.

"What? Say it."

"Your cock. I want your cock in me. Please."

"Put your legs around me." When she did, he said, "That's my girl," and slowly, carefully entered her. "You're so snug, so hot. You feel amazing." Finally, with long, slow strokes he filled her completely. Then he stopped.

"Oh, God, don't stop!" She arched against him, angling her hips, moving restlessly.

"Tell me what it feels like, sweetheart," he whispered as he nuzzled her neck.

"Good. It feels good."

"No, tell me *really* what you feel."

"I can't feel anything but you. Every part of me just feels you. I've never... . . . . I never knew... . . . " She took his face in her hands and kissed him with a hunger only the taste of him could satisfy.

When he began to move inside her again, her internal muscles contracted around him as her climax revived and strengthened. He thrust faster, harder. His breathing matched. "Come with me, babe," he said in a hoarse voice.

But he didn't have to ask. The second orgasm overwhelmed her and brought on his as together they rode it out to completion.

Afterwards neither of them spoke as they lay twined together trying to get their breathing and heart rates back from someplace in the stratosphere. Finally, he said, "So, was that *nice* for you?"

She nipped him on the shoulder. "You win. You're amazing. I never—"

He stopped her with a quick kiss. "Babe, it takes two to be amazing. And we were, weren't we?"

"Yes, but I'm not a babe."

"Believe me, sweetheart, you are a babe." He touched the tip of her nose with his index finger. "A babe who owes me twenty bucks."

"Are you serious?" She reared her head back and threw him a startled look.

"A bet is a bet. And you just admitted I won."

"I've never paid for sex before." The startled look had morphed into a disingenuous smile. "Is a check okay?"

"If the purpose of that comment was to put me in my place, it sure as hell worked."

"You don't like being a boy-toy?"

"I guess you didn't notice that's not in my personality." He kissed her again. "But, maybe for you, I'd be willing to give it a shot." After a few minutes of contented silence, he said, "About that bad-in-bed thing . . . "

"Okay, can we leave the subject behind? I've conceded just about everything. What more do you want?"

"Alsace-Lorraine. East Jerusalem. Fifty-four Forty or Fight."

"What, were you a history major or something?"

"We just did 'or something.' And, no, political science." He snuggled her close to him. "But now that I think about it, there is one other concession."

"The Korean DMZ?"

"Nice, but not what I had in mind. Concede that you feel better about not sending me away with just a goodnight kiss. You do feel better, don't you?"

"You make it sound like this was some kind of pity fuck to improve my mental health."

He laughed. Loudly. "What do you know about pity fucks?"

"I may not be the most experienced person in the room, but I have impeccable sources who are quite knowledgeable on the subject of sex. So, was this one?"

"Not unless you took pity on me for being so pathetic when you rejected me." He dropped a kiss on her head. "What else have you learned from these sources of yours?"

"Well," she said, running her finger over his mouth, "I hear that some men can have sex more than once a night."

He pulled her hips against him where she could feel the already impressive beginnings of another erection. "You have excellent sources, sweetheart. And they are correct."

Chapter 6

"Isn't it the guy who's supposed to fall asleep after sex?" he asked when she opened her eyes. He was watching her, his head propped up on his hand, a grin on his face.

"Sorry, I must have dozed off." She tried to hide her embarrassment by nestling her face into his shoulder. He wouldn't let her.

"We've only made love twice and you're already bored with me?"

"Hardly. I'm tired from working in the gallery. Maybe that's it. Although, truthfully, it's been a long time since . . . you know . . . and you're quite a bit more intense than I'm accustomed to so maybe . . . "

"Then I'll take it as a compliment." He brushed hair away from her cheek with the back of his fingers. "You're even beautiful when you sleep."

"I've always been afraid I drooled or slept with my mouth open and my tongue out or something equally disgusting."

"Not that I noticed." He turned toward the side of the bed.

She kissed his shoulder. "If you want to go back to your hotel room, it's okay."

"You trying to get rid of me?" His back was to her so she couldn't see his eyes.

"No, I'll understand if you want to leave, that's all."

"And if I want to stay?" He turned to face her and she could see he did.

"I'd like that."

"So would I." He sat up on the edge of the bed. "But I'd love something cold to drink, first. Can I get some ice water from your 'frig?"

She started to sit up. "I'll get it for you."

"Let me. You go back to sleep."

She pulled the covers up around her shoulders and made a soft sound. "Okay, if you don't mind."

"I'll be back in a few minutes."

"I'll probably be asleep when you get here."

*

He put his boxers on, went to the kitchen, and got a glass of ice water. Returning to the bedroom, he made sure she was asleep, then went into her office. A half-hour later he checked on her again, pulled his cell phone from his jacket pocket, and went down the steps to the entryway where he made a phone call.

"David, it's Michael."

"What the hell are you doing calling at this hour of the night?"

"You want to know what I found or not?"

"Do you have them?"

"What I have is nothing. I've been through her desk, all her computer files, and her file cabinets. She doesn't lock the cabinets or any drawer in her desk. Her computer isn't password protected. None of the files are either. She's not hiding anything."

"You didn't find any financial files at all?"

"Yeah, I found all her personal files, copies of their IRS filings, the records for her gallery. Nothing like you told me she had. This is a wild goose chase."

"How'd you get into her office at this hour?"

"Don't ask."

"So, the old girl fell for the young man's flattery."

"She's not old and don't talk about her that way."

"Am I hearing this right? Are you finally falling for someone? I don't believe it."

"Fuck off, David. All I'm saying is she doesn't deserve what I just did to her."

"Right." A sigh came from the other end of the line. "Okay, if you're sure. I guess you're going to have to figure a way to check out his files."

"No. I said I'd do this one last thing for you. I'm not doing—"

"Maybe you can use the same talents with him you did with her. I hear he swings both ways."

"Shut the fuck up. I'm done."

"Michael! Don't hang up . . . "

He hung up.

When he crawled back into bed, she stirred and curled up close to him, her hand on his chest. The gesture felt trusting, almost childlike. He put his arm around her and cursed himself, his former partner, and the client from hell who'd put him in this position.

*

She woke with a start, breathless. God, what she would give to dream like that every night. Blinking at the daylight making its way through the sheers on her bedroom window, she stretched. It was morning. No more dreaming. Time to get to work.

Funny, she felt sore in interesting places like she'd . . .

Then she remembered. Not all of it was a dream.

But she was alone in bed. The pillow next to her was cold, although it smelled of him. Had he left after she'd fallen asleep the second time? Why hadn't he wakened her to say goodbye? Maybe he changed his mind about staying . . . about a lot of things. Oh, hell, she'd been foolish to think . . .

"Good morning, sweetheart." Dressed only in his boxers, he appeared in the doorway with two mugs in his hands, coffee, from the smell. "Guess I won't have to tempt you awake with this."

"Oh, are you up . . . ah . . . awake?" She was staring at the front of his boxers and could feel herself blushing as she stumbled on her words.

He grinned at her embarrassment. "For about half an hour. I thought breakfast in bed might be nice." He sat next to her and handed her one mug. "However, you need to do some serious grocery shopping. This is about all I could manage in the breakfast department other than the coffeecake and scones leftover from yesterday, and I wasn't sure how you felt about stale crumbs in bed."

"This is great. Thanks. I apologize for what's not in the kitchen. I've been eating take-out for weeks while I work on the gallery." She sat up, pulled up the sheet to cover her breasts, and took the mug. "I thought maybe you'd left. Gone back to the hotel so you could get an early start for home."

"Without saying goodbye? I wouldn't do that." He watched her as if waiting for something from her. "Anyway, I don't think I'm going to leave Portland for a couple more days."

"Oh." A pause. "That's nice." A race to find another word. "I mean, I'm glad." She sipped at her coffee, not looking at him. "Will you stay at your hotel?"

"I imagine I can if I want to."

The pause was longer this time and mutual with much coffee sipping and no talking. Then, looking up at him, she said, "You could stay here."

He put the mug on the bedside table, stripped off his shorts, and hopped over her to get back in bed. "I thought you'd never ask."

She finished the coffee and put the mug beside his. "Good." Feeling mischievous she said, "I mean, I have one man helping me, but another one would let me finish the to-do list for the gallery faster."

"I have another kind of to-do list in mind." He pulled the

sheet away from her and tugged at her arm to get her to lie down again. "Can't you take a couple days off?"

"Assuming I get a lot of work done today, I guess I can. And what would you have on your to-do list?"

"While I waited for the coffee to brew, I got to thinking that you've probably always made love in bed and always in missionary position. Right?"

Nodding, she felt another blush redden her face. "Are we going to spend all our time together talking about sex?"

"No, sometimes we'll be *having* sex." He ignored her eye roll. "Okay, so, since that's true, there are lots of opportunities here for me to be your first and I thought we could explore . . . "

"Actually, you already have been my first."

"Right. Betting on sex. Or do you mean paying for sex?"

"Neither one. Well, yes, both. But that's not what I meant."

He frowned. "Then what . . . wait, are you telling me you never had an orgasm before?"

"No, although it was more like a sneeze before and with you I'm sure it registered on Portland State's seismograph. Anyway, that's not it either. Last night, you kissed me . . . where . . . ah . . . where no one ever has before. I liked it. More than liked it. Loved it."

"Good, one thing checked off already." He smiled. "Surely those 'informed sources' you told me about have talked about other interesting things. And maybe there are places where you've thought about making love but never have."

"What, you're going to catalogue my fantasies and then check them off like a perverted Christmas list?"

"Hmmm. I'm Santa and you're the naughty-or-nice little girl. That could be fun. Although I'm a little uneasy about the perverted part—you're not talking about involving animals or innocent teenagers, are you?"

"If I do this, and that's a big *if,* you'll be the youngest and the only other person involved. And animals? Dear God, I can barely handle my own species. I sure as hell have no desire to add another."

He roared with laughter.

"Not so loud. I just heard Jamie come in downstairs. He'll hear you."

"Who's Jamie?"

"The guy I told you about who's been helping me get the gallery ready. When we're dressed, we'll go downstairs and you can meet him."

"In a bit. First . . . " He nudged his erection against her thigh. His fingertips touched her breast, his breath feathered over her lips. "I can't seem to keep my hands off you."

"Mmmm. Having your hands on me is one of the things I like about you."

"What else do you like about me?" He pulled her leg up over his hip and touched her sex.

"Just about everything right now."

A long while later, they showered and dressed. She'd chased him out of the bathroom when he wanted to make love in the shower and disentangled his arms from around her when he suggested sex in the kitchen as the best way to start the day. Saying that they'd already made love more in the last twenty-four hours than she had in the whole previous year, she asked his patience until she got used to it.

He turned serious, held her, and told her she would never again, as long as he had anything to say about it, be without someone to make love to her whenever she wanted. She bit her lip to keep tears from forming.

With the key to her apartment in his pocket, Collins left to check out of his hotel, snagging a piece of leftover coffeecake on his way out the door.

Liz poured what remained in the coffeepot into her mug and wandered into her office. Sated with sex and deficient on sleep, she didn't trust herself to remember what needed to be done today. The master to-do list on her computer would tell her what had to be finished before she played hooky with Collins.

But even her lust-fueled brain knew something wasn't right when she sat down at her desk. For starters, her wireless mouse was on the right side of the keyboard. She was left-handed and used it on the other side. And the art books she'd just bought from Powell's. They were no longer on the desk, but in two piles on the floor. Looking around the room she saw other signs that someone had moved things. More books out of place. A file cabinet drawer slightly open. Who the hell had been in here?

It had to have been Jamie. He was the only other person with a key to the apartment. Well, Mason had access to it, too, but he was never here. And Collins had spent the night, but he had no reason to be in her office. It must have been Jamie. But why? She heard movement downstairs in the gallery. She'd just go find out.

He didn't give her much time to ask about her office. "Sooo . . . " he said with a smile and a sideways glance, both of which looked suspiciously leer-like. "You weren't alone when I came in this morning, were you? I heard two people walking around upstairs and heavy footsteps coming down the back stairs a while ago."

"Jamie, I hate to have to ask this but . . . "

"Was it morning after or early morning delivery?"

She could feel her face redden. "Obviously I should think about carpeting everything upstairs." She pushed through her embarrassment. "Look, I have to ask you something."

"From your face and this need to change the subject it's certainly interesting, whichever it was."

"If you'll let me ask what I need to, I'll satisfy your curiosity."

"Deal." He held out his hand for a handshake, but she ignored it.

"Did you go up into my apartment for something yesterday while I was gone?"

His hand dropped and she could tell from his expression that she'd hurt his feelings. "Of course I didn't. I wouldn't go into your place without asking you beforehand. Why are you asking?"

"Stuff got moved around in my office. I just wondered if you needed access to something about the gallery and . . . "

"I would never invade your space like that. I wasn't even here yesterday. We went to a matinee of *A Chorus Line* and then dinner." He was looking her straight in the eyes and all she saw was how hurt he was that she thought he'd do something like that.

"I don't mean to sound distrustful. I apologize. I just can't figure it out. You have the only other key. And the only other person around was . . . " She stopped. "I'm sorry. I must have done it myself." Shaking her head to clear the suspicions, she changed the subject. "Was it a good production of *A Chorus Line?*"

"Mason said he'd seen better but I loved it." His indignant look had softened somewhat, but he still sounded like a hurt puppy.

She put her arm around his shoulders. "I apologize again. Forgive me?"

"I'll think about it. If you satisfy my curiosity about your overnight guest." That sounded more like the real Jamie.

"He'll be back in a while and you'll meet him."

Jamie put up his hand for a high-five. "It's about time. All you've done since you bought this place is work. I was beginning to worry you'd forgotten how to play."

"Then you'll be happy to hear that I'm going to take the next couple days off. Since I won't be here, you can stay home, too, if you'd like."

"No, it's perfect timing. This'll give me the chance to set up the inventory and billing systems and update the website. We have images from all your artists now . . . "

"Except for the new one. I'll ask him for . . . "

"You signed someone else? Who?"

"A metal sculptor named Collins."

"You signed Collins? Oh my god, Liz. How did you manage? Oh my god, is that who . . . ?"

"You know who he is? Am I the only person in Portland who didn't know?"

"Don't be so hard on yourself. You know everything about what hangs on the walls. I know more about what sits on the pedestals. Collins is one of the hottest new sculptors in the region. But you didn't answer my question. Was that who I heard tromping down the steps?"

She shook her head, trying to find a way to avoid telling him the truth. When she realized she couldn't, the headshake changed to a nod. "Yes, it was but . . . "

"This is sensational. Wait 'til Mason hears."

"Jamie, please. I don't want this spread around. First of all, it may be nothing, just a one night—few nights—thing. In the second place, if people think I sleep with artists to get them to sign with me, I'll be the laughing stock of the city."

"I promise I won't say a word to anyone except Mason. And he'd never do anything to damage your reputation so he'll keep his mouth shut."

"You both better keep your mouths shut. Now, before I can take off for that downtime you think I need, we have to get the hanging system reinstalled and some more work done on the pedestals. If you'll drag out that ladder for me, please, I'll work in here and you can keep painting."

A half-hour later, Jamie was in the storage space working on display pedestals and Liz was on the ladder finishing the installation of the last section of the hanging system that would eventually display the paintings of her artists. She was about to climb up one more rung when she felt someone caress the calf of her leg.

"The logo for this gallery should be you on a ladder. It's sexy as hell and would sell a lot of art," Collins said as he climbed the first two rungs of the stepladder and circled her waist with his arms.

"How is it you seem to appear out of nowhere when I'm on a ladder?"

"You leave the door open for me. Now, let me get you off this. I want to kiss you." He lifted her from the ladder and stepped to the floor with her. He was in the process of making good on his promise when a discreet cough came from behind them.

"Sorry to interrupt but, Liz, you said you wanted all the rest of the pedestals painted. Even those short ones we weren't sure you'd need?" Jamie asked.

Liz extricated herself from Collins's embrace. "No, not those little ones. I think I'm going to get rid of those." She waved her hand in Jamie's direction. "Collins, this is Jamie Bruce. He's the reason I can even hope to be ready for the opening in October. Not only is he willing to do whatever it takes to renovate the place, but he's a genius with websites and social media. Jamie, this is Collins."

The younger man held his hand out to the sculptor. "I'm so excited you're going to exhibit here. I'm a big fan of your work. That piece you have in the bank building downtown, 'The World on a String.' It's fabulous."

"Thanks. It's one of my favorites, too. Couldn't believe a bank would buy it. And you do websites? Really? I want one but I've never gotten around to putting it together."

"I'd love to help you. You can take a look at Liz's to see my work. Which reminds me, I need images from you so we can get them up on the site."

"I'll take care of that when I get back to the cabin. And,

Liz, don't get rid of any small pedestals until you see what I'm bringing for you. Smaller ones might work for a couple pieces I've got in mind. They might even look good in one of your windows."

"Oh my god, that's excellent," Jamie said. "I've been worried about what we were going to put in the windows. Your work would be perfect to draw people's attention." And with that the two men began to plan the window displays, the website for Collins, and the fate of the universe, for all Liz knew.

At the end of the day, the hanging system was reinstalled on all the gallery walls, the pedestals were painted, the small temporary walls were erected, and the card rack and print bins placed. Jamie shook hands with Collins before he left and hugged Liz, telling her to enjoy her days off. She asked him to say hello to Mason when he got home.

The door had barely closed behind the young man when Collins said, "Mason? He knows Mason?"

"He lives with him."

"That's who Mason left you for? Sweetheart, you're a helluva lot more forgiving than I would be."

"It's odd, I know. But when Mason suggested it, it was hard to say no. He—Mason—has been so wonderful about giving me advice, free services—he did a whole advertising campaign for me, printed the brochures, paid for the ads."

"But didn't it seem awkward?"

"A little, at first. But then I discovered Jamie has great taste, knows a lot more about three-dimensional art than I do, and he's a genius with computers. That's what he did for Mason's company. Besides, I like him. For a while I even thought of him as the son I never had, but then the ick factor kicked in and I went back to thinking of him as the sweet-young-thing who works hard, gets along with me, and lives with my ex-husband."

"The more I know about you, the more I like you, Liz

Fairchild."

"Which is certainly better than the opposite reaction."

She tidied up; he got his bag from the car. When she'd finished changing clothes, they went down the street to her favorite café. He'd insisted they go out to eat, saying he knew what was in her refrigerator and it didn't look promising.

After they'd ordered their meals, she asked, "So, what's the real reason you wanted to eat out tonight?"

"Why would I have a reason other than your empty refrigerator?"

She raised an eyebrow and stared at him over her wineglass.

"Okay, you're right. I want to talk about my to-do list and figured if we stayed in your apartment, we'd get distracted and never get it started."

"You're not serious about that, are you?"

"Of course I am. So, first, tell me five places where you'd like to have sex."

"I can't do that. It's too embarrassing."

"Yes, you can. I'm going to count to ten and then you'll give them to me."

"Collins . . . "

He held up his fingers, one at a time. "One . . . two . . . three . . . four . . . "

"I'm not going to . . . "

"Five . . . six . . . seven . . . eight . . . "

"This is ridiculous . . . "

"Nine . . . ten . . . go." He dropped his hand as if starting a race.

"Umm . . . the beach . . . a forest . . . a hot tub . . . someplace public." She felt exhausted by the effort.

"That's only four."

"Oh, hell. I don't know . . . the back seat of a car, maybe." Breathing hard, she slumped back into her chair.

"I knew you could do it." He rubbed the palm of his hand across his cheek. "The only one that might be a challenge is the last one. I'll have to think about that a bit. I'm six-four and you're six—"

"Five-eleven."

His smile mocked her attempt to correct him. "Like I said, I'm six-four and you're six feet tall and in most cases the back seat of a car would be, well, uncomfortable, let's say." His hand reached across the table for hers. She could feel his foot rubbing up the back of her calf. "We can start on the list tomorrow. Or today. If you're game we could check off number four right now."

She snatched her hand back from him. "I didn't mean this public."

"Just trying to see where the boundaries are, babe."

Chapter 7

The following morning, Collins was out of bed before the alarm went off. He dressed, brought Liz coffee, and took off, telling her he had errands to run and some business to take care of before they got on with their plans. When she asked questions he pretended it was all a big secret for their two days together. The truth was, he couldn't tell her the details of what he was doing.

His guilt about going through her office had begun to eat at him even while he was doing it and it had gotten worse over the past twenty-four hours. Not only did he like her more than he had expected to—maybe *like* was too weak a word, come to think of it—but the more he learned about her relationship with Mason, the more sure he was that there was nothing she would do to hurt him. Even if she could. Which he doubted.

He was beginning to believe that David's client was a lying scumbag and Mason Fairchild was the good guy in all of this. But that was David's problem. His was how to deal with what he'd done. He'd come up with an idea that might get him off the hook, both with Liz and with David.

All he had to do was get it sorted out before she figured it out. And sell it to David.

As soon as he was out of Liz's apartment, he called L.A.

"So, Michael, how's it going up in the Rose City? It's beautiful here." His former partner was terminally cheerful in the morning. It was one of the only things Collins disliked about him. "You going to cozy up to the old guy today? Find his books for me?"

"I told you, David, I'm through playing spy for you."

"What, you afraid you'll fall for him, too?"

"Fuck off. But I do have an idea about how we can get this sorted out."

"I'm listening."

Collins told him. After a brief argument, David agreed to let him try. But if it didn't work, they were headed for court with or without the books. The client was adamant.

*

After Collins left, Liz felt nervous and confused. Part of her realized she'd actually be doing something she'd fantasized about, but another part wished she could back out of it. What had she been thinking, giving him that list? She knew he meant it, that he'd find all those places, and then she'd have to live up to what she'd suggested. A beach? Sand in places where sand doesn't belong. A forest? Twigs, leaves, and bugs in places where they don't belong. A public place? Dear God.

The back of a Volkswagen was easy and a hot tub tame after the other three.

When Collins returned, she asked him how his errands had gone. He shrugged off her question, not saying much. The man from last night who'd been so eager to fulfill her fantasies seemed to have disappeared. She was confused. Had he gotten a dose of common sense about it? Absorbed her fear? Cooled to the idea?

He went up and down the stairs a couple times, making phone calls in the parking lot out back. She got more curious—and more concerned—as time went on. But just as she was about to ask if he wanted to reconsider the plan for spending two days together, he seemed to shake off his mood. He hugged her, kissed her cheek, suggested she change into jeans and running shoes, and pack for overnight. They'd be leaving in a half-hour, he announced. He disappeared down the steps again with his duffle bag without telling her where they were going.

It became obvious when he headed west on the Sunset Highway that they were going to the coast. The sand option. Great. And, on top of it all, in spite of being the end of summer, it wasn't warm enough to lie naked on a blanket on the beach. This just got worse the more she thought about it.

At least he'd let her pick out the music. She still loved the songs she'd played as a young teenager. She listened to mix tapes from three decades ago in her house and always kept at least one Eagles and one Chicago CD in her car at all times.

Today, however, Rod Stewart singing "Maggie May" was up now. Next came Creedence Clearwater Revival, who would accompany them to the coast.

And then, the fun would begin. The fun. The embarrassment. The sand. What the hell had she gotten herself into? And why was she continually asking herself that question about this man?

"Okay, it's obvious where we're going. Which beach?" she asked about an hour into the trip as she was changing CDs.

"There's a state park south of Cannon Beach that's in a beautiful woods. And it has a secluded beach. I have a campsite reserved for us. Because it's a good fifteen-, twenty-minute walk to the ocean, it's usually pretty deserted especially—"

"Oh, no, I'm not rolling around in the sand right near a state park. I was thinking more like an out-of-the-way . . . "

"Okay, then the campsite it is."

"A public campsite? Are you crazy?"

"Relax. I went up to REI this morning and got a tent. We'll be in the woods, in sort of a public place, in a tent . . . " He glanced at her and laughed. "You look absolutely terrified. This is going to be even more fun than I imagined."

He was right about how beautiful the park was. And, because it was the middle of the week and the middle of the day, the crowd was sparse. That didn't make Liz any less nervous. She tripped over tree roots as she tried to help put up the tent, finally leaving it to him to complete while she looked around anxiously, trying to see how close anyone else was to their campsite, sure that it wasn't remote enough.

After the tent was secure, they walked hand in hand to the beach carrying the two blankets Collins insisted they needed and a picnic basket. Near the top of the dune, he stopped so they could look around. He was right again. The beach was even more deserted than the campground had been. Not a soul in sight.

"This looks like a good place," he said after they crested the dune. He spread out one of the blankets where they'd be hidden among clumps of beach grass, kicked off his shoes, and helped her remove hers.

He'd brought an elegant lunch. Cold game hens, a thermos with basil-infused, roasted tomato soup, marinated green beans, grapes. After he'd laid out all the food, he produced two plastic champagne glasses and two bottles of wine to go with them.

"Did you think it would take a couple bottles of champagne to get me to participate in your little plan?"

"It may have occurred to me. But if you don't want to drink any wine, that's okay. Your call."

She held up her glass for him to pour some of the bubbly into it. "Well, maybe just a little. I like champagne too much to turn it down."

They toasted each other and she grudgingly admitted that he'd found as romantic a spot as she had imagined. At his urging, she lay back propped up on his thigh. He served her lunch, feeding her green beans one by one, popping grapes in her mouth, refilling her glass once, then twice. As they finished their meal, the sun broke from behind a line of clouds and streaks of sunshine began to dance over the ocean waves, looking as lighthearted as Liz felt.

After they finished lunch and Collins tidied up the remains of their meal, he lay down across the blanket from her. He didn't try to touch her, just continued their conversation about beach trips they'd taken as kids in California. When she couldn't stand the suspense any longer, she said, "Okay, now what? Aren't you supposed to, I don't know, make a move here or something?"

"It's your fantasy, sweetheart. You're going to have to decide what's next."

"Suppose I decide to take a nap?"

"Then, take a nap. Like I said, your fantasy, your move."

She reached across the blanket and touched his cheek. "On second thought, maybe I'd rather have you hold me."

"I can do that." He moved toward her, snugging her hips against his. "What now?"

"Well, if you won't kiss me, I guess I'll kiss you." She brought her mouth to his. He tasted of wine and salt air, sweet fruit and desire—her tongue sampled all of it. When they came up for air, she touched his mouth. "God, I love kissing you," she whispered.

"Anything else you love doing with me?" he asked.

She inched her hand slowly down his chest until she reached the waistband of his jeans. "Yes, now that you mention it, there is." She unsnapped and unzipped him. After he returned the favor he spread the second blanket over them so they could wriggle out of their jeans and undies.

"I thought we were . . . " she began as he pulled her close.

"You think too much."

"But you said . . . "

"Talk later. Fantasy now." He illustrated his point with his mouth and his body.

*

Still covered by the blanket, they slowly came back to Earth after sweet lovemaking. She played with the curl that fell onto his forehead and asked if a little boy with a curl in the middle of his forehead was like the little girl with the curl.

"No," he responded. "When she was bad she was horrid. When I'm bad I'm wonderful."

They were working up to round two in the sand when

suddenly the breeze picked up. In fact, it was getting very windy, as if a storm were coming in. Which seemed odd because the sun had gotten steadily brighter while they were there.

Collins sat up to look out towards the horizon. He started laughing so hard she had a difficult time understanding what he was saying. Finally, he got out, "Your fantasy. The Coast Guard. They're in it?"

"The Coast Guard? What are you . . . ?" She bolted upright and got the answer to her question before she had it finished. Hovering just far enough away so it didn't swamp the couple with the backwash from the rotor blades, was a Coast Guard helicopter. The two Coasties inside the helo were waving at them.

"Oh, shit. This is awful," she said, pulling the blanket further up over her before dropping her head into her hands.

"They're too far away to see us clearly enough to know who we are. What's outside the blanket is dressed and what isn't dressed is completely covered. It's really kinda funny."

"Easy for you to say. Here I am . . . "

"I'm here, too, babe. And all they can see is a couple having a little afternoon delight on the beach. They're either impressed that a white-haired old guy can still do it or they're jealous because they're working and we're not. Maybe both."

"Right. Working. My tax dollars being used to spy on me."

"You sound like one of those anti-government nuts."

"Good God, I hope not. But I am embarrassed."

"Because they'll what . . . report you? To whom?"

"Because they'll film us and put it on YouTube."

"But I don't see anyone hanging out the side of the copter with a camera in hand, so I don't think that's gonna happen. Come on, they won't leave until we acknowledge we see them. We'll wave; they'll go away."

He waved and, reluctantly, so did she. Just as Collins predicted, as soon as they did, the pilot and his—or her—

colleague flew seaward until their helicopter looked like an oversized dragonfly in the distance.

When they'd gone, Collins pulled Liz to him and kissed her forehead. "So, we've got beach and public place checked off the list, haven't we?"

"And added 'with an audience,' too," she said.

"I don't think they actually saw anything, Liz."

"But they'll have a good story to tell their buddies when they get back to base."

"I doubt it's the first time anyone's made love on the beach, babe. Maybe they just amuse themselves by keeping count."

Twenty minutes later, as they finished the last of the open bottle of champagne, two helicopters appeared from the south. This time, the couple was completely dressed and sitting up on the blanket.

"Looks like we have more company," Collins said as he waved at the approaching helos.

Liz laughed and joined him in greeting their new friends. With nothing interesting to see, the Coasties waggled their aircraft at them in salutation and went on their way.

Once the helicopters disappeared, Collins started packing up the picnic basket. "I think we've done everything that can be done here, don't you?"

"Hell, yes. And so help me God, if I show up on YouTube or Facebook or whatever else is out there to torment foolish old women . . . "

"And so help me God, if you don't stop harping on your age, I'll take the damn videos of you half-dressed myself and post them." He held up three fingers in the classic Boy Scout sign. "Scout's honor."

"I didn't know you were a Boy Scout."

He abruptly dropped his hand and grabbed the bag they were using to collect trash. "There've been times lately I wish I was more Scout-like than I am but, no, I've never been a Boy Scout." He walked away from the blanket, picking up random bits of trash and adding them to the bag.

It was the second time today he'd abruptly pulled away from her. She couldn't figure out what she was doing to make him draw back. She hadn't been kidding when she said she felt inept in dealing with men. Maybe this was the result of falling into bed with someone she'd known for such a short time. Perhaps this had all been a mistake. She didn't want it to be. But what the hell was going on?

When she caught up with him she took the bag he was holding and put her empty plastic glass in it. "You must be a Boy Scout if you're intent on policing the beach like this. Need some help?"

"No, I can . . . " He looked at her, seemed to register her concern. "Sorry. Got some other stuff on my mind."

"Is there anything I can help with?"

His expression turned sad. "No, no. It's fine. Just a business deal." He held her close. "But you don't deserve a distant lover. I'll work on being better." He took her hand and they returned to pick up the blankets and picnic basket.

It wasn't exactly the free and open communication she'd hoped for, but at least he was back with her. For the moment.

As they slid down the dune towards the heavily wooded campgrounds, Liz asked, "Are we staying overnight in the tent?" She hoped the answer would be no, but was willing to be a good sport if that's what he wanted to do.

He smiled. "What would you do if I said yes, sweetheart?"

"I'd be gracious and acquiescent. And probably not like it very much."

"That's what I thought. You didn't strike me as the camping type. The tent was just so we could get a site and maybe a temporary place for us if the beach didn't work out. I made another reservation down the road at a motel with spa suites and a good restaurant close by."

"Are you planning on checking off all five of those things in two days?"

"I'd only planned two. But maybe we can get to four if I can find a nice forest on the way back tomorrow."

"When did you say you were going back to the Wallowas?" She shook her head. "If I have any chance of surviving to get my gallery open, it better be soon."

After checking "hot tub" off Liz's five places they went to dinner at the four-star restaurant across the street from their motel, where they had another long evening of engaging conversation. Aside from finding him an adventurous—to understate the obvious—bed, bath, and beyond partner, she was learning to appreciate other aspects of Collins. He was, of course, interested in her work and loved discussing art. But he also had an interest in almost everything else—movies, theater, sports, politics, international issues.

He talked warmly of his family and was interested in hearing about hers. The only blank space in his conversation was his life as an attorney in L.A. He wouldn't talk about it. He dismissed it as over and done with, not worth mentioning. She couldn't help wondering if it was connected with his distracting business but she was afraid to ask, afraid to take the chance she'd drive him away with her curiosity.

She couldn't remember when she'd met someone she enjoyed being with as much as she enjoyed him. His sense of humor meshed with hers. They had similar tastes in restaurants, wine, and food. He was interested in everyone from the sommelier in the white-tablecloth restaurant to the ranger at the state park. He loved her music, thought she had a great eye for design and paintings (although he told her, with a smirk, she needed to brush up on the three-dimensional arts), and shared her love of spy movies and thrillers.

He was, in short, so damned perfect she was afraid if she wasn't careful she could fall for him. She didn't know which was worse, the idea that she might begin to love him or that she could lose him.

The morning after their beach adventure they slept in. Then they grabbed coffee and scones at a nearby bakery before taking the long way home, back up the coast to Astoria before heading east to Portland.

Jamie was still at the gallery when they arrived. After Liz inspected the new inventory and billing systems he'd finished, as well as the updated Facebook page and their new Twitter account, Jamie showed Collins his proposed template for the sculptor's website. They got into such a detailed discussion that Liz left them to it and went upstairs. A half-hour later she heard the gallery door close and Collins's footsteps on her stairs.

*

Before he left the next morning, Collins promised to send images of the work he'd be bringing her and to call her as soon as he got home. Although she held him for a long moment before he got in his car, she wasn't devastated by his leaving. She knew he'd be back for the opening. And having him three hundred miles away gave her a chance to take a deep breath and figure out exactly what the hell had just happened to her.

He called when he got home and told her he missed her. In spite of her suggestion they text instead of phone, he called every night during the weeks they were apart. He needed to hear her voice, he said, needed to tell her how much he missed her, person to person.

He also told her he was pushing up his return date—he'd be there the weekend before the gallery opening. And he asked her not to make any plans for the Monday after he arrived because he'd made some plans of his own for them. She thought he came

71

close to saying a lot more at several points in their conversations. But, unable to deal with both complications in her personal life and the mountain of last-minute details for opening her business, she pretended she didn't understand what he was talking about. He let the subject drop.

Chapter 8

The Sunday before her gallery opening, Liz was inspecting the wall on which she'd just finished hanging a series of photographs of Portland when she got a weird feeling on the back of her neck, as if someone were outside, watching her. People walking past had been glancing in as she hung the work of her artists, but this didn't feel like a random curious onlooker.

It wasn't.

Collins was outside talking on his cell. He had an expression on his face she'd never seen—tense, focused, almost grim. Pacing up and down the sidewalk, he gestured wildly with his free hand, sometimes with his free middle finger. As she watched, he looked in, noticed she'd seen him, turned his back to her, and walked out of sight without any greeting.

Five minutes later he was standing outside the gallery window again, his arms crossed over his chest. On his face he wore his best cocky, arrogant Collins grin. Wearing jeans and the black T-shirt she loved—okay, honestly? she lusted after what was under the shirt—he was apparently sure she'd eventually realize he was there so he hadn't bothered to knock.

"What was all that pacing about?" she asked as she opened the door.

He didn't answer but drew her hard against him, kissing her. No sweet and tender kiss, it was hungry, fierce, and demanding. It said how much he'd missed her. How much he wanted her. Releasing her, he said, "God, I'm glad to see you."

"How long were you outside and who were you talking to on the phone? You looked almost mean."

"It's just business. Nothing you have to worry about."

"If you tell me not to worry my pretty little head about business, I'll deck you."

He looked as if he might be about to say something serious to her, but he backed off. Or, more accurately, moved in closer to drown her curiosity in another kiss. She tried to keep her question in mind but, once again, she found it impossible to think while he was kissing her. She got lost in his arousal, and her own, heat and warmth pooling in her belly as her body melted and molded to him. She couldn't breathe, she couldn't think, the questions were lost.

When he released her mouth, she held onto him, clutching his arms. "Dear God, you do things to me I don't understand," she said, close to gasping for breath.

He continued to hold her close. "You have no idea how much I've missed you, sweetheart. If we weren't standing in front of two walls of windows, I'd already have you stripped and flat on the floor."

"But we checked off 'public place with an audience' the last time you were here, so we don't need to do that again." She could feel him smile against her temple.

"Right. No need to check off anything more than once, is there?"

"No, like Stephen Sondheim says, 'I Never Do Anything Twice.' "

"Oh, yes, you do."

"All right. Apparently for you, I'm willing to make exceptions." She disentangled herself from his arms. "But I want my gallery to be known for the work my artists show, not what I and one of my artists show of themselves. Let me get closed up here and we can . . . " She paused as she locked the front door. "Oh, wait. What about your work? Where is it? Let's get it into the gallery before we go upstairs."

"It's all in the back of my pickup."

"A Porsche and a pickup? Interesting transportation options."

"Ever try lugging metal sculptures around in a Porsche?" He

followed her out the door. "When we're finished unloading, how about the café down the street for dinner? I'm starved."

"We can eat in. I was very domestic this past week. Made it to the grocery store, put clean sheets on the bed." She cocked her head and frowned. "I guess I should ask before I assume—are you staying with me?"

"Where the hell else would I stay, babe?"

By the time they'd unloaded Collins's truck, Liz had proof that in addition to whatever else she knew him to be, he was truly a talented artist. He'd brought eight pieces. Two were small cast bronzes of fishing boats on stormy seas. Two, the larger pieces for the window displays he and Jamie had designed, were abstract renderings of grasses with wildlife and insects hidden in them. The other four were representations of old Frank Sinatra songs. They were part of the series, he explained, that "World on a String," the piece Jamie had admired, belonged to.

Liz saw how Collins viewed the world and she loved it. All of it.

*

Later that night he started to get out of bed.

"Want some ice water? I'll get it for you," she said.

He looked chagrined for a moment. "No, that's not it. I brought something for you. I was going to give it to you Thursday but I can't wait that long. It's in my duffle bag." When he came back to the bed he had his hands behind his back.

"I kept obsessively thinking about you and thought maybe if I worked it out in sculpture, I could move on to other work. Didn't make any difference. I still obsessed about you. But I did end up with this." He brought from behind him a grapefruit-sized, ball-shaped object. At his urging she sat up and took it from him.

It had three parts. The outer part was a hollow ball, created of metal wire that had no apparent pattern to it and no indication of how to get into an inner hollow ball that was a swirl of metal ribbons enclosing the final bit, a thin, metal piece shaped like part of a jigsaw puzzle.

She laughed with joy at the toy-like nature of the work, rattled it so it made a noise, inspected it from all angles. "This is amazing. How did you do it? Why did you do it? What's it called?"

"I told you why. So I could stop obsessing about you. And how I did it is my secret. It's called 'Liz' because it's you. A puzzle wrapped in mystery inside an enigma."

"Isn't that how Winston Churchill described Russia?"

"Close."

"Why do I remind you of Russia?"

"You don't. But that does represent how I think of you. You present yourself as someone who's upfront when in fact, very little of the real you is obvious—and there's hardly any way to figure out who you are from what *is* obvious. That's the outside enigma. The mystery is why this woman ignored—or denied—how passionate she was for so long. And the puzzle at the center of it all is where she wants to go from here."

She could feel tears well up in her eyes as she turned the object in her hand and listened to his explanation. "I don't understand how . . . you barely know . . . no one has ever . . . " She swallowed the lump in her throat before looking at him.

"Liz, I love you. I've been trying to tell you over the past weeks, but you kept changing the subject. That's how I know you. I love you."

*

After a couple hours of moving and rearranging pedestals, sculptures, and window displays, the perfect presentation of Collins's work still eluded them. Well, eluded Jamie and Liz. Collins had been happy with the display for some time. Finally he said he was leaving, once again, to attend to some business.

"Wait, before you go, we need to talk," Liz said as he headed for the door. She saw the uncomfortable, stunned-bunny look on Jamie's face when he heard the dreaded "we have to talk" and suggested he take an early lunch.

She didn't have to make the suggestion twice.

As soon as Jamie was gone, she took a deep breath and jumped in. "Collins, what the hell's going on? You keep making these mysterious phone calls and disappearing for hours at a time and coming back in a shitty mood. I deserve to know what it's about."

He didn't meet her eyes. "Liz, I can't . . . "

"Are you thinking about leaving my gallery and going with someone else, someone more established?"

"Why would I go with someone else when I'm perfectly happy here?" Now he was looking straight at her.

"You could have your pick of any gallery in town. Why did you come here?"

He dropped his eyes before he answered. "I liked what I saw when I came in. A new gallery suited me."

Something didn't track with that answer, but she couldn't put her finger on it.

"Well, are you seeing another woman? I mean, we never talked about that. If you want to see other people, I certainly can't object but I should know, particularly if you're sleeping with her . . . "

He wrapped her in his arms. "Sweetheart, I'm not sleeping with, eating with, talking with, or hanging out with any other woman. You're all the woman I want." He pulled back and gave her that stormy look that melted her insides. "The business I'm dealing with isn't about where my work is or another woman. I promise. I'm sorry it's been distracting. But I think it'll be taken care of in a few days and we'll never have to worry about it again." He kissed her forehead. "Now, I have to get out of here. But I'll be back about 4:30. Be ready to leave for dinner at five and wear a dress."

He'd brushed it all off again even though he had technically answered her questions. There was nothing more she could think of to do. She sighed. "Okay. Five. Five? Isn't that early for dinner?"

"It's a bit of a drive to the restaurant." Another kiss. "See you then."

After he left she tried to make sense of their conversation. He was telling the truth. She was sure of that. But she was equally sure there was more to it than he'd said. She just didn't know what to do about it.

So, to put it out of her mind, when Jamie got back, she threw herself into the final round of musical pedestals, hung the last paintings, and organized the display of jewelry. On Tuesday, she'd get the wine and snacks for the opening reception and pick up the brochures for her design business from the printer. Then everything would be set for the "soft" opening on Wednesday, when Liz hoped to have enough visitors come through the gallery to see how the flow of people worked and whether she had to make any changes before the official opening on First Thursday.

The details of getting her business off the ground had driven her—and been driving her—crazy for months. Tonight, assuming Collins came back in a good frame of mind, she hoped to focus on something more enjoyable.

A quick shower, some time in her bathroom with a hairdryer and her makeup, and she was ready to slide into one of her LBDs. She had three little black dresses. One, flattering but conventional, was what she used to wear to Mason's business dinners. One was suitable for funerals. The third was flat out sexy. She picked the third. Maybe it would guarantee Collins would be in a good mood when he saw her in it.

The A-line skirt stopped just above her knees. The form-fitting front was cut up to her neck, the back plunged almost down to her waist. The sleeves were long and tight. She never wore much jewelry with it, just gold stud earrings and a couple slender bangle bracelets. She planned to wear her favorite black ballet flats, but hadn't put them on when Collins arrived back in the apartment.

"If I ask you nicely, will you wear that dress every time we go out?" he asked as he came into the bedroom.

"I'm glad you like it. It's my favorite." She turned to the mirror to put in her earrings and heard his quick intake of breath when he saw her bare back.

"Wow. I was wrong. Not every time we go out. Every day of your life." He kissed her between her shoulder blades and ran his hands around her waist, holding her close to him so he could nuzzle her neck. He let her go with another kiss on her back and she grabbed her shoes. But he shook his head as she slipped on her ballet flats. "No, you should wear heels with that."

"I hardly ever wear heels unless I want to tower over everyone and dominate the room."

"Wear them tonight. You can't possibly own heels that will make you taller than I am, if that's what's worrying you. And you should have figured out by now that I'm not easily dominated."

She dug into her stack of shoeboxes and brought out a pair of black sandals with two-inch heels. When she put them on, he nodded in approval.

"Now all I have to worry about is finding something to wear that measures up to my date's outfit." He was changing into the gray trousers, black T-shirt, and jacket he'd worn to the dedication.

"You managed to pick up a few groupies wearing that the last time you were in town. It should work for a quiet dinner, don't you think?"

Just as he finished dressing, his cell phone rang. "We'll be right there," he said to the caller. He ended the call and stuck the phone in his pocket. "Your chariot awaits, my lady." He opened the door at the top of the steps and followed her down.

A limo was idling by the curb. The driver opened the passenger door as they approached. She turned to Collins with a smile. "A limo? Is this . . . ?"

"We're going to the Long Beach Peninsula. I wanted to have wine with dinner and not fall asleep at the wheel on the way home. Besides, you and that dress would look silly in a pickup truck."

"Long Beach, as in the Washington coast? What's there?"

"The Shelburne Inn. You'll love it. The food's great. So's the wine." He opened the door for her and walked around to talk to the driver while she settled herself. As he got in the car with her, a smoked glass window dividing the space between the driver and the passengers rose, giving them complete privacy. The limo pulled out from the curb just as Collins popped the cork on a bottle of champagne. He handed her two crystal flutes.

"What're we celebrating?" she asked as she held out the glasses for him to fill.

"Isn't it obvious? I found a home in Portland for my work and it's at the exciting new Fairchild Gallery. We're both going to be famous." He touched his glass to hers in a toast.

Although she was a little disappointed his answer wasn't something more personal, she smiled. "Maybe not famous. Maybe just well known in Portland," she said before she took a sip. "Actually, let me amend that. You're already well known in Portland. With luck, I'm about to catch up."

He opened a basket she hadn't noticed until then and brought out a cutting board on which he arranged crackers and a small bowl of caviar. He put a teaspoonful of caviar on a cracker and held it to her lips. "I don't like all the stuff people serve with this, I like mine straight. I hope you don't mind."

"In Russia, they say all you need is ice-cold vodka or chilled champagne. I think you've got it covered." She took a bite. "Oh, God, this is as good as . . . "

"If you say as good as sex, I'll be crushed."

"I was going to say as good as I had in Russia, but it's almost worth it to lie just to see what you look like crushed."

*

It took two hours to drive to the restaurant. After a two-hour dinner of superb seafood and the perfect wine, he escorted her back to the limo for the drive home, impatient to get to dessert—the real dessert he'd planned for the end of their evening.

"You were right. It was worth the ride. That dinner was wonderful. Thank you," she said as the driver headed off for Portland.

"The night's not over yet, babe," he said, taking her hand and nibbling at her fingers. "We have two hours to enjoy before we get home."

"What do you have in mind?"

"You haven't asked why I wanted you to wear a dress."

"No, I wondered but . . . "

Instead of answering her unfinished question, he pulled her leg over his lap then lifted her so she straddled him, her knees alongside his hips. Running his hand up her bare leg, he pushed the dress up to her hips. "I wanted to do this all the way to the restaurant, but decided to save you for later." He crushed her mouth with his, one hand at the nape of her neck, the other under her dress, around her bottom, holding her so close there was a good chance the silk of his T-shirt and the fabric of her dress had merged into a new fiber.

When he broke the kiss, he could tell she was becoming aroused. Her voice shook as she said, "I thought the reason for the limo was so you could drink at dinner."

"I didn't say it was the only reason, did I?" He grazed the back of his hand across her breasts and felt her nipples harden. When he nipped at them with his teeth, she sighed. His hands slid up under her dress, his fingers slipped between her legs. The heat of his hand met the heat of her body and he thought something might actually catch fire.

Tugging at the band of lace at the top of her bikini panties, he whispered, "We need to get rid of these, sweetheart. Help me."

She slipped off her shoes then raised herself on her knees and he slid her bikinis down her thighs. When she sat on his lap again they struggled to get the panties off one leg, then the other. She was giggling by the time he accomplished the task, but when he went back to kissing her and ran his hands up her bare thighs, she moaned instead, her eyes glazing over in a haze of desire.

His hands stopped at her hips, his thumbs just touching the now-damp curls between her legs. She fumbled with his belt, impatiently tugging at the button and zipper on his trousers. He took her hands, slowed her down, and helped her unbuckle his belt.

When his zipper was down, she released his erection from his boxers. Before he could stop her, she slid from his lap to the floor of the limo and, kneeling between his legs, wrapped her hands around him.

"Liz, what . . . ?" He lost his thread of the sentence as she started licking up the side of his shaft and sucking him gently. "Oh, babe, you don't have to . . . "

When she looked up, her green eyes were dark with a desire that matched his own. "I want to. Please. Unless I'm not doing it right . . . "

His cock jerked in response and he barked out a laugh. "You're doing just fine."

She guided the head of his penis into her mouth, sealing her lips over the glans. When he groaned and touched her head, she took more of him in, sucking and tonguing him.

It was the sexiest thing he'd ever seen. She may have been inexperienced, but her hot breath and warm mouth, her soft tongue on his hard cock was more erotic than anything he'd ever felt. She looked triumphant, as if she were not only sexually engaged but feeling powerful because she could give him this pleasure.

The tiny groans and moans she made resonated in her mouth, vibrated against his flesh, driving him rapidly toward climax. From those sounds and her rapid breathing, she was as excited as he was. At least he hoped she was because he didn't think he could take much more of the rhythmic pull of her mouth on him without exploding, and he was sure she wasn't ready for that. Not in the back seat of a car in her favorite black dress.

He pulled her up from the floor back onto his lap. "Wasn't it good?" she asked. "Did I do it wrong?"

"Way too good, babe. But I want us both to be in this."

She straddled him, on her knees again, as he lowered her onto him, entered her, knowing it wouldn't take long to reach a conclusion. His mouth fastened on hers in a rough, punishing kiss, his fingers found her most sensitive spot and massaged it until he felt her muscles convulsing around him and she flew apart in his arms. She bit at his neck as he gripped her hips and surged into her, claiming her as his. Because she was. Now and always, his.

She nestled against him, but they realized quickly that the back seat of a car, even a limo, was not the place to cuddle in afterglow. Particularly not when the lights of I-5 were appearing outside and the ride—the one in the car—was almost over. They cleaned themselves up a bit, rearranged their clothes, panicked when they couldn't find her panties until he located them inside the champagne bucket. By the time they were back in Northwest

Portland, they were reasonably sure they had everything under control.

When they got into the apartment he followed her into the bedroom and they both looked in the mirror. Her lips were swollen from kissing, her face was blotchy with whisker burn, and her hair had lost the sleek, sophisticated look it had when they'd left the restaurant. He had a love bite on his neck and his curls looked like they'd been blown up in a chemistry experiment gone awry.

Liz grinned at his reflection. "All I can say is, I hope you tipped him well enough that he'll keep his mouth shut."

Chapter 9

The "soft opening" did what Liz hoped it would do. She found out where the lighting didn't work and refocused a couple pin spots, and she moved one of the small temporary walls to make it easier to navigate through the gallery. By the next day, everything was set for the official opening on First Thursday, the monthly art event when galleries opened new shows and hosted evening receptions to introduce their artists.

Everything was set except Liz. She couldn't eat breakfast, couldn't even drink her coffee. She spent the morning changing her mind a half-dozen times about what to wear, how to position the wine and snack tables, and where to put the e-mail sign-up sheet. The gallery was due to open at noon and she still hadn't made up her mind or eaten anything, so Collins called in backup.

Jamie arrived to staff the gallery while Collins took Liz to the café down the street for a big bowl of chowder and bread, a lot of bread. By the time she returned to The Fairchild—the art critic for the daily newspaper had shortened its name to that—her blood sugar had stabilized and she was able to focus on what needed to be done.

At five, when the first after-work visitors came through the door, Liz was in hostess mode. Dressed in a vibrant blue caftan, adorned with a necklace one of her artists had created and a pair of earrings Tinkerbell and her pals could have used as hula hoops, she greeted everyone who came in. Pouring wine and introducing her artists to visitors, she appeared to be presiding over the biggest party in the city instead of opening a new business in the middle of a recession.

The gallery enjoyed a steady stream of sales early in the evening—small pieces of her ceramic artist's work, jewelry, a couple prints, notecards. Then Mason and Jamie arrived.

Jamie had raved so much about Collins's work that Mason wanted to be the first to purchase a piece of it from the new gallery. It was a two-fer for him—he pleased the person he loved and helped the person he still cared for. While he and Jamie were deciding what to purchase, another couple began considering which piece they would buy. Liz could sense a competitiveness as they went from piece to piece, each couple carefully eyeing the other.

Finally, the man and woman chose a cast bronze boat and Jamie selected one of the abstract grass pieces displayed in the windows.

Liz thanked Mason as she wrote up the sale. "You didn't have to do this. You've already done so much to make the business work."

"I'm doing it partly for you, but mainly because it makes Jamie happy. He loves working here with you. He was never this excited when he was doing IT in my office, I can tell you."

"I've been thinking about offering him a paying job. Would that be okay, I mean, I don't know how you feel about it . . . "

"Actually, I was going to talk to you about that. He asked me last week if I thought you were going to hire staff and I said your business plan didn't include paid staff for a year at the earliest. He was disappointed. So I was going to ask if you'd reconsidered that decision." He put up his hand to stop her question. "And, no, I didn't say anything to him about it."

"Of course you didn't. But I have changed my mind. After spending all my time here for the past however many months, I have a new appreciation for small business owners. I think I'd rather dig into my savings in the short run if I have to and hire someone take a couple shifts a week to give me some breathing space."

"Good move. You don't want to burn out."

"So, what would you recommend for compensation? I'm thinking $15 to $18 an hour."

"That's a lot for a sales position and an inexperienced salesperson."

"But he does all the computer work, too."

"Offer $15 and a review in six months when you see how the business is going. It's not as if he needs to support himself."

"Mason, I know how generous you are but believe me, I also know how nice it is to have your own money. He's worth paying for."

"I know he is. But I don't want you to get in over your head."

"Okay, I'll make it $15 for now, more as we grow. I'll talk to him tomorrow." She handed him the credit card slip to sign. "And can we keep his present in the window until Collins replaces it?"

"Of course you can. After all, Jamie'll get to see it when he works, won't he?"

The sale of two of Collins's pieces seemed to open the floodgates. Soon a third piece sold. Liz's favorite watercolor of a spring scene in the Chinese Garden left after hanging on the wall a mere two days. Her oil painter got a commission for a family portrait. She lost track of the number of unframed prints the photographer sold. Jamie had to pitch in to help her write up the sales.

Among the people who bought from her were two women Liz had met recently at a luncheon hosted by a local civic organization. Fiona McCarthy was a reporter for the weekly alternative newspaper, *Willamette Week*. Her buddy, Margo Keyes, was an assistant district attorney. The two women had been out to dinner and stopped by the gallery to give Liz moral support.

Seeing that the crowded gallery was doing just fine, they turned their attention to the art. Fiona found an unframed photograph of the St. John's Bridge on a misty morning, a view she saw often from her kitchen window. Margo bought the necklace Liz was wearing, but laughed off the idea she'd ever wear the hoop earrings that went with it. Both women complimented Liz on the gallery she'd created with her good taste and promised to come back with their friends.

Busy with sales and her visitors, Liz didn't get as much chance to observe Collins interacting with the crowd as she would have liked. What she did see was fun to watch. He was friendly and warm, answering the same questions all night long with a freshness to each response that made the questioner feel like the only one who'd ever thought of it.

More than once during the evening, their eyes met across the gallery and she knew he was watching her as closely as she was watching him. He'd smile, his gray eyes zapping her with a private look that made her want to close the gallery and run upstairs with him where they could be alone.

One odd thing occurred. After Liz commandeered Jamie to help her write up sales, she saw Collins and Mason off in a corner having what looked to be a serious discussion. She hadn't even known they'd been introduced. *What the hell was that all about?* she wondered.

By the end of the evening, a case of wine had been drunk, several wheels of cheese had been nibbled down to nothing, a number of boxes of crackers and countless bowls of pretzels and nuts had been consumed. But she'd sold more than $9,000 worth of art, most of that amount from Collins's work. The Fairchild Gallery was off to a great start.

*

After closing at nine, they tidied up and took care of the money. Liz, who'd sworn she was so wired she wouldn't be able to settle down, was asleep before Collins joined her in bed.

He was the one who lay awake in the dark, staring at the ceiling. She nestled against him, as she often did in her sleep, her hand on his chest, making him feel protective, making him feel like he just might want to build that damn white picket fence and get that golden retriever after all.

But before he bought dog food or hit the home improvement store, he had to talk to her. Now that the problem was taken care of and the gallery was open, he'd run out of reasons to put it off.

Tomorrow. He'd tell her tomorrow.

Chapter 10

She woke with a feeling so warm and wonderful she wanted to bottle it to save for the inevitable rainy day. Curled in a ball with her eyes still shut, she replayed the evening in her mind to make sure she remembered it correctly. When the rewind was complete she knew she was right. It had been a success. If last night was any indication, she had a shot at making it as a gallery owner.

With the opening out of the way, she could face something else. Collins and what she felt for him. It went far beyond gratitude for the major part he'd played in her success last night. No man had ever filled her with such joy, such happiness, such passion. Nor had any infuriated and driven her crazy, too, but that seemed to be the other side of the passion coin, as far as she could tell. He'd told her one time that he loved her, but hadn't said it since. Maybe he was waiting for her to respond in kind.

She opened her eyes and rolled over to tell him, to hear him say again that he loved her. But he was gone.

The note he'd left in the kitchen said he had business to finish up and would be back by ten. She showered, dressed, and went downstairs to the gallery to finish getting everything ready for Jamie to open at noon. When Collins returned at 9:30, she was back in the apartment, sipping coffee and tabulating sales from the night before.

"Look," she said, waving credit card receipts. "It's over $9,000—mostly from sales of your work. You'll have a great check from The Fairchild Gallery by the end of the month." When he didn't respond and just walked past her to the kitchen, she put the paperwork down and followed. "You left so early this morning," she said, trying to kiss him.

"Yeah, I had something I had to finish up." It was happening again. He came back from taking care of his "business" and was distant, distracted. "Is there more coffee?"

"Just made a fresh pot. Let me get you some." She got a mug from the cabinet.

He took it from her and poured coffee from the pot. "I've got it."

"Did something go wrong?"

Sipping from his coffee cup, he avoided her eyes. "I need to tell you something and I'm not sure how to do it."

She couldn't breathe. "Is it as serious as it sounds?"

"I guess that depends on how you react when I tell you."

"Okay, then let's get it on the table."

He walked to the living room and sat down on the couch. Waving her to a place next to him, he said, "Sit, please." He took her hand and tried to lace his fingers through hers, but fumbled. "This is hard for me to say."

"Please don't tell me you're gay or married."

"I think either one might be easier than what I have to tell you."

She withdrew her hand from his and wiped it over her face. "Oh, God. Then just spit it out."

He pulled himself up straight and looked her in the eye. "You asked me why I picked your gallery and not a more established one. I was looking to strike up an acquaintance with you."

"You were . . . what? An acquaintance with me? Weren't you looking for a gallery for your work?"

"No . . . well, yes, in a way. But not exactly." He shook his head in frustration. "How do I explain this without sounding . . . ?" He stared up at the ceiling for a few moments then returned to looking at her. "When I left L.A. my old law firm was doing okay. But less than a month later, three of the senior partners bailed and then a bunch of the associates left. It seemed like once I'd pulled out everything crumbled. I ended up doing contract work for David, the partner who was left to clean up the mess."

"Can we cut to the explanation of how this relates to coming into my gallery, please? You're making me nervous."

"I'm getting there." He took another sip of his coffee. "After maybe eight, ten months, David finally stabilized things and I thought that was the end of my helping him. Then about six weeks ago, he called and said he had a new client who wanted to sue a business associate and I was in a unique position to get the information he needed to make the case. He said it would be the last time he'd ask for help. He said I owed him. And I felt I did."

"I'm still not clear . . ."

"The person his client wanted to sue was Mason. David's client swore that if we asked Mason to show us his books, we wouldn't get the truth about how he'd cheated his clients. He said there was a second set of books with the real figures. But they weren't kept in Mason's office." He stopped, looked at her, then finished. "They were supposedly in the possession of Mason's ex-wife who might have been using them for her own purposes."

She closed her eyes as his words hit her. In agonizing, painfully slow motion, everything in the life she'd recently built began to crack and break into tiny pieces.

"You came into my gallery to seduce me so you could find out where I hid Mason's imaginary books?" She could barely get the words out in a whisper. "You thought I was a blackmailer?"

"No, Liz, no. Of course not. I came in to get to know you, find out if you could help me, help David's client. I wasn't there to seduce you. And I had no idea I'd fall in love."

"Stop it, Collins. You came to use me, to discover my vulnerabilities and use me."

"No, that's not what I was doing. I was doing a favor for a friend. After I met you, I tried to get out of it, but he played on my guilt about leaving him. He asked me to . . . so I . . ."

"You what? What did you do? Tell me the rest."

"You weren't the bitter divorcée I was told I'd find so I didn't think you'd hand over what you had, if you had anything. So David asked me to look in your office for Mason's books."

"My office. Here? In my apartment?"

He nodded, his eyes averted.

"You went through my desk? My files? My computer?"

"Liz, please . . . "

"Answer me."

"Yes, I went through it all."

"When?"

"What does it matter?"

"It matters to me. When?"

"The first night I . . . "

"Jesus. You're the one who moved everything around, aren't you? And I blamed Jamie." She slumped, like a balloon with the air slowly leaking out. "You went through all my things and have been lying to me ever since."

"I've never lied to you. I didn't tell you what I'd done, but I've never lied to you."

"So a sin of omission is okay, is it? Maybe in your lawyer's world it is, but it doesn't work that way in mine." She straightened up again, her shoulders pulled back and her chin out. "I thought I'd been used by the best, but you beat Roger and Mason hands down. And for what—money?"

"No, that's not why . . . I was only . . . "

"Stop. I don't want to hear any more excuses." She took a deep breath, her hands fisted in her lap. "At least poor Mason was struggling with his own demons when he used me. And Roger thought he was making me a better person and himself a better teacher. Oh, wait, of course. That's what it was. I was your project. Are you writing a book on how to give sex lessons? Do you want me to write a blurb for the jacket?"

"I deserve every bit of your anger but please, I can make this up to you if you'll let me. Give me a chance to show you how sorry I am, how much I love you."

Earlier she would have given anything to hear him say those words. Now the sound of them nauseated her. "Sorry? Sorry couldn't begin to cover what it would take to make this up to me." She stood up. "Pack up whatever you have here and leave. Now. I can't look at you anymore."

He reached for her hand. She backed away. "Do. Not. Touch. Me."

"Please, Liz, I've tried to make it right. I didn't mean to—"

"What can you possibly do to make this right? You bulldozed your way into my life, into my gallery, into my bed, so you could violate my privacy, my trust, and you think this is some sort of . . . what? . . . social faux pas you can make right with your charm and a few more lies? Well, you can't. All you can do is get the hell out of here."

He stood with his hand out, still trying to reach her, unable to make the connection. Finally, he went into her bedroom and returned a few minutes later with his bag.

She opened the door at the top of the steps. "I'm invoking the termination clause in our contract. As soon as it's up, I want your work out of my gallery. Sooner, if you want to take it. But deal with Jamie about removing it. I don't want to have anything to do with you." She glared at him, feeling the tears backed up in her eyes, determined not to let him see them.

He stood at the open door, his gray eyes suspiciously shiny and certainly sad. "I never meant to hurt you, Liz. I'm more sorry than I can say that I did." He took a step through the door. "I wish you'd—"

"Know what I wish? I wish I'd never met you." She shut and locked the door. When she heard the downstairs door slam, she went to her bedroom and gave into the tears she'd been holding back.

Chapter 11

Someone was at the outside door to her apartment leaning on the buzzer and annoying the hell out of her.

"Whoever's there, stop that. Go away. I'm not seeing anyone right now," she yelled into the intercom, not caring how rude she was.

"It's Mason. I want to talk to you. Let me up or I'll stand here pushing this buzzer 'til it breaks. Then I'll go back home and get Jamie's key."

She hit the release for the door. "What the hell do you want?" she asked as he bounded up the steps.

"Nice to see you, too, Liz." He pushed past her into the living room. "Jamie's worried about you. He said he hasn't seen you in two days, since the reception. I have a feeling I know what's going on so I came to see if I could . . . " He seemed to register her for the first time. "You look awful."

"Thanks, is that why you're here? To tell me how bad I look?" She made a pass at pushing her hair back from her face, realized how sticky it felt from leftover product, and gave up. "And what do you mean, you know what's going on?"

"This is about what Collins told you, isn't it? It's my fault you're upset, or rather, my business's fault. He's been working to get it straightened out. What he's done could probably get him disbarred but he got—"

"I'm not interested in the business dealings of someone about whom I couldn't care less, thank you very much."

He looked like he was suppressing a smile. " 'About whom I couldn't care less'? You're really pissed, aren't you? You only talk like that when you're beyond ticked off. So, I'm right. This is about Collins. But, Liz, I may deserve to have you lie to me, don't lie to yourself. You care, all right. One hell of a lot."

"Mason, you don't know what you're talking about which, I grant you, is unusual. Guess there's a first time for everything."

"Sit." He gently pushed her down onto the couch. "Would you like some coffee? A cup of tea? I'd offer to make you something to eat, but Jamie said he didn't think you'd been out of the apartment since the reception. Knowing you, you've been working so hard you haven't exactly stocked the refrigerator with decent food."

"I don't want anything other than to be left alone. Could you manage that, do you suppose?"

"I'm making coffee and then we're going to talk." He disappeared and when he returned, she could smell the coffee brewing. "Okay. Now you're going to listen, my stubborn friend, whether you want to or not."

"This doesn't concern you."

"Of course it does. If that asshole client hadn't decided I'd padded my billings and sent David Starr off on a hunt for my mythical second set of books, you'd be downstairs working in your new gallery, happy with a modestly successful opening. Of course, you'd have never met the love of your life—"

"He is not the love of my life. He's a deceitful, sneaky bastard who used me."

"Liz, listen to me. You're feeling sorry for yourself, looking dreadful, and about to make the biggest mistake of your life when you should be—"

"If this is meant to buck me up, it is not working."

He had a look on his face she recognized as frustration. "I've never been very good at getting through to you when you're like this, but I am not going to give up like I used to. So, please stop talking for a minute so I can think."

She laced her fingers together, positioned them on her knees, and perched on the edge of the couch, saying nothing.

"The innocent schoolgirl look doesn't exactly suit you. But thanks." He ran his hand over his bald spot. "Let me come at it this way—Collins called me a couple weeks ago and told me about this jerk of an ex-client who decided we charged too much for advice he didn't like about how he had to change the way he did business. Collins thought he had a way to get it settled out of court. Friday morning, after we finalized the agreement, he asked my advice about how to tell you what he'd done. I said just be honest. You were a forgiving person. Hell, you'd forgiven me. I told him you wouldn't be happy, but you'd understand."

"Wrong again. That's twice in less than ten minutes. Must be a record for you."

"Apparently I underestimated the unhappy part and was dead wrong about the understanding part. You're determined to be angry at him, aren't you?"

"I'm determined to make sure I never get used like that again." She stood up. "Look, it's very kind of you to go to bat for Collins. If that was part of the price he exacted for getting the whole thing settled with his client, then you've done what you were asked to do. But it's not going to make any difference. So, you can report back that you tried and failed." She walked to the door and opened it. "Thanks for coming by. And for making coffee."

He hesitated beside the open door. "I didn't come because I had to. I came because I wanted to. I care for you. You know that. And I want to see you happy."

"I'll be happy when I don't have to deal with that man ever again."

Mason cocked his head and squinted his eyes. "Methinks the lady protests too much."

"Don't go all Shakespeare on me. You know I hate it when you do that."

"Then try this: Did you cry this hard when I left?" Before she could answer, he held up his hand. "Don't bother sparing my feelings by saying you did. I know that's not true. You were hurt.

You may have been embarrassed. But you weren't devastated. You and I didn't have what you and Collins have. That's why this has hit you so hard, because you love him so much. Anyone can see that. When you're with him, it's like the rest of us don't exist."

He kissed her forehead. "It comes along very rarely, Liz, something like you two have. I should know. I found it with Jamie and was willing to turn my whole life upside down because of it. You'd be a fool to throw this away. He did something wrong. He knows that. He's ready to do whatever you want to atone for it."

"Fine. Then he can go back to the Wallowa Mountains and leave me alone. That should work."

"I know you can be stubborn but I've never seen you this unwilling to listen. You're usually the first to accept what's clearly in front of you. The truth is, you love a man who made a mistake doing a favor for a friend. That makes him human. Just like the rest of us. Even you, Liz." When she didn't respond, he said, "Okay, I give up. But I'm still concerned and I'll be checking on you later if we don't hear from you." He left, closing the door quietly behind him.

She went back to the living room, trying not to cry. That's all she'd done for two days, that and try to get some sleep. It had worked in reverse. She couldn't stop crying and she hadn't had a decent night's sleep since Thursday. This morning she thought she'd gotten the tears under control, but now Mason had started them up again. Damn it.

Damn his interfering, too. He simply wasn't right. Couldn't be right. After fifteen years, you'd think he would know her, but apparently he didn't. This wasn't because she loved Collins so much. She hated him. Didn't she? He'd done nothing but hurt her. Hadn't he?

Of course she'd made mistakes. But never ones that caused other people pain like this. Well, maybe leaving college and running off with Roger had hurt her parents. And his children. But weren't they all okay with it after? Damn it. Damn it. Damn it. This wasn't about her and Mason couldn't turn it into that.

He was wrong about another thing, too. She could forgive. She'd done it a lot. As he bloody well knew. This wasn't her fault. Collins had been the one who lied. Okay, maybe he hadn't lied. Maybe he had just kept it from her. Right. Kept from her the fact that he only came to her gallery so he could weasel information out of her about her ex-husband.

Actually, he'd never asked her anything about Mason. Even when she'd talked about their marriage. Still, that was also the same night he . . .

Enough. The pity party had to end. Collins wasn't worth it.

An image skittered through her brain of him feeding her grapes that day on the beach, in the perfect romantic spot for a picnic. That was quickly followed by the memory of his face in the back of the limo as he toasted their mutual success. She could hear his laugh, smell his aftershave. Her memory was as treacherous as her body. He was imprinted there, too.

Remembering only brought on more self-pity. She needed something to get her mind off him. Some fresh air. A walk. Maybe coffee. She'd start with the pot Mason had made.

After a cup of coffee and an attempt to tame the rat's nest in her hair, she started toward the stairs to go out for a long walk. The metal orb Collins had made for her caught her eye. That had to go. She'd put it away in her desk downstairs and make sure Jamie gave it back to Collins when he came to pick up his work.

As soon as she walked into her gallery she realized her mistake. Everywhere she looked she saw Collins's work, saw how he understood the world and expressed what he felt. His compassion for the crew in the fishing boat, tossed in the storm-racked sea as they fought the implacable ocean, was evident. In the two pieces in her windows she saw his sensitive depiction of the life hidden in the prairie and she knew he understood the high plains were more than just a lot of tumbleweed and dried grass. And the Sinatra pieces. Oh, God, the Sinatra pieces. She'd never thought to ask him how he came to be such a fan of Old Blue Eyes, but she loved the work he'd done to honor the late singer.

He hadn't done the easy ones—not "New York, New York" or "Chicago." No "High Hopes" with the images of the ant and the rubber tree plant. He'd picked love songs. "How Deep Is the Ocean?" combined the seas from the fishing boats with heart-shaped sea creatures yearning for the sky. "Strangers in the Night" had twisted, elongated figures of a man and woman whirling in their first dance. "Put Your Dreams Away" combined a box of clouds, hearts, and a figure closing the lid. Her favorite, "Fly Me to the Moon," depicted a couple climbing through a whirling coil of star-studded metal to reach the moon.

How could someone who created those pieces be so insensitive?

She answered her own question. He couldn't be. He wasn't. Collins was not the kind of man who would set out to hurt her. He'd done a favor for a friend that had gone wrong.

Just like Mason said.

She looked at the metal ball in her hand. He'd known her less than a month, yet he understood her inside and out. Knew what made her tick. Understood how to woo her, how to win her, how to love her. Where would she ever find that again?

What the hell was she going to do about this?

The sound of the back door to the gallery opening interrupted her thoughts. She must have left it unlocked when she came downstairs. Without looking around she said, "Back already, Mason? If you're here because you forgot to mention one of my shortcomings or remembered something else to say about how awful I look, I'm not sure I'm up for it."

"It's not Mason, sweetheart. It's me."

The Collins who stood there was not the cocky, self-assured man she'd known. Lines she'd never noticed before etched worry across his forehead. His eyes were smudged with dark circles, as if he hadn't been sleeping either. His shoulders slumped in defeat before she even spoke.

"What are you doing here? How did you get in?"

"The back door was open. I'd just pulled into the parking lot when I saw you come downstairs. I've been here every day hoping to see you." He put out his hand to her. "Please, Liz. Can't we talk about this?"

"There's nothing to talk about."

"Yes, there is. I hurt you, I know, but I love you. Please." He walked toward her, his hand still out. "I've never begged for anything in my life but I'm begging you—let me show you I can make this right."

She covered her face with her hands as fresh tears fell. When he closed the remaining space between them she didn't have the energy to back away. He tentatively put his arm around her and, when she didn't resist, he pulled her close, kissing her hair.

"I only ever wanted to make you smile. You've had enough tears in your life. And now I've gone and done this by messing up like I did." His hand gently massaging her back felt so soothing, so consoling.

"If you'll give me another chance, I swear I'll spend the rest of my life making this up to you." He studied her face, frowned as if what he saw wasn't what he wanted to see. "If you tell me to go, I'll leave. But I'll be back. And I'll keep coming back until you say you'll give me another chance—if it takes me a hundred trips."

She hiccoughed a laugh between sobs in spite of herself. "That's how you operate, isn't it? You keep coming at me until I finally give in and do what you want." Slowly she pulled away from his embrace. "But not this time. I'm not . . . I can't . . . it hurt too much. I trusted you and you . . . " She shook off the hand he tried to put on her shoulder. "I have to think about this, about what Mason said . . . "

"Mason? What'd he say? Maybe he was right, maybe—"

"Stop. Just stop. I need time. I need . . . I don't know what I need other than for you to go now. Please, just go." She disengaged from him, trying to keep the tears from sliding down her face.

"I said I would go if you asked me to, so I will. But I'm not leaving Portland until we talk. You know how to reach me. And if you don't call, I'll be back." He took her hand and pressed a kiss into the palm. "I love you, Liz. That isn't going to change. Ever."

When she heard the back door to the gallery close, she ran up the steps to her apartment, still crying. Why the hell couldn't she stop? It must be because he made her mad. But he looked so sad and unhappy just now, not like the confident Collins she knew. This Collins looked like he needed someone to hold him and tell him it was going to be all right. If he hadn't hurt her, she'd be the one doing it. Putting her arms around him. Kissing his sweet mouth. Letting him kiss her back. Listening to him tell her he loved her. Telling him she loved . . .

Oh, God, telling him she loved him. All the tears in her body couldn't wash away the simple fact that she loved him. Probably always would.

This was a hell of a time for her ability to face the truth to return.

She stood inside the door at the top of the steps to her apartment, realizing what she'd just done. He said he loved her. But did she really think he'd keep trying when she'd so adamantly pushed him away, not once but twice? She loved him, but she'd never told him so. Was it too late? She had to go after him, to find out.

Throwing open the door, she barged through, almost pushing him backwards. They would both have tumbled down the stairs if he hadn't grabbed her arm and then the handrail.

"Whoa, where are you—where did we both almost go—in such a hurry?"

"What the . . . ? I heard the back door close." She rubbed her eyes like a child to clear away the few remaining tears.

"It broke my heart to see you crying like that. I couldn't leave. The gallery door was still open so I came up the steps from there. I was just about to knock on the door." He bracketed her face with his hands. "That's what I was doing. What are *you* doing?"

She sniffed back the last tear. "I decided I might as well avoid the hassle of throwing you out a few dozen times and give in to the inevitable. Save myself some emotional turmoil."

He enveloped her in his arms and breathed out a huge sigh. "Thank God. You know I would never give up. Not when it comes to you." He pulled back, then lowered his head and gently, very gently, kissed her. Without lifting his mouth completely from hers, he said, "I love you. I'm sorry I hurt you like this. But I never will again. I promise."

She grabbed his arms and dug her nails in. "You're damn right you never will. I'll never let anyone use me again. Ever. Not you or anyone else. Do you understand?"

"I understand, sweetheart. If I ever do anything that feels like I'm using you—other than maybe for great sex—you have my permission to remind me of this conversation." He winced as she gripped his arms tighter. "Although the scars on my arms from your nails will probably do the job."

"We have not yet reached the point in this apology where you can joke about it." She released her grip on his arms, but wasn't sure what to do with her hands.

"Tell me when we get there, will you? I love to hear you laugh." He tried to guide her arms around his waist, but she still stood stiff and unyielding.

Closing her eyes and dropping her forehead to his chest, she said, "You drive me crazy, you know that."

"In only the best ways, I hope." He lifted her chin and kissed her again, this time not so gently.

Giving up all pretense of resisting, she relaxed into his arms, where she realized she'd wanted to be all along. "Mason said you did something that might get you disbarred. Is that true?"

"He's exaggerating. I didn't betray any lawyer/client confidence. Just brokered a settlement between the two parties. No big deal. I thought if I got it cleared up, you might look kindly on me and forgive what I'd done."

"Mason was pretty impressed by it."

"Then he's easily impressed." He brushed his mouth across hers again. "Can we go into the living room? The stairwell's a little cramped."

When they got to the couch, he held her for a long moment. "So, we okay here?"

"We're getting there."

"What can I do to get us closer?"

"I need to take a shower and wash my hair. And I need some sleep, maybe something to eat. Then we can talk about it."

"How 'bout I take care of you for the afternoon? Let me wash your hair, get you some food, and rub your back so you can sleep."

"You don't have to."

"But I want to. Let me."

She did. He ran a tub full of hot water, knelt by the side, and washed her hair. Then he dried her with one of her thick, luxurious towels and wrapped her in a cashmere robe. After she eaten the grilled cheese sandwich and tomato soup he fixed for her, he coaxed her to the bedroom and tucked her under the covers. He lay down beside her and rubbed her back until she was on the edge of sleep.

Drowsy, curled up on her side, she asked, "Will you be here when I wake up?"

"Where else would I be?"

"Getting your things from the hotel."

"They're in the car. I've brought them with me every day. I'm an optimist."

Her laugh was soft and sleepy. "You're the most maddening man, Collins."

"It's Michael."

That brought her back from the edge of sleep. "What's Michael?"

"My name. It's Michael Collins Thompson. I avoided Wolf Tone Thompson, which is what my brother's saddled with. Our parents admired Irish patriots."

She smiled. "You didn't have to . . . "

"It's my last secret. And yes, I did. If I can't trust you with that, how can I expect you to trust me?" He kissed her. "I love you, Liz."

Reaching up to touch his face, she whispered, "Thank you. And I love you, too—Collins."

www.ingramcontent.com/pod-product-compliance
Lightning Source LLC
Chambersburg PA
CBHW010644100726
47900CB00011B/2960